The Lightning Jar

The John Simmons Short Fiction Award

The Lightning Jar

Christian Felt

University of Iowa Press · Iowa City

University of Iowa Press, Iowa City 52242
Copyright © 2018 by the University of Iowa Press
www.uipress.uiowa.edu
Printed in the United States of America
Interior design by Sara T. Sauers

The University of Iowa Press is a member of Green Press
Initiative and is committed to preserving natural resources.
Printed on acid-free paper

"The Smallest Cousin" first appeared in the *Tishman Review*,
April 2018.

Library of Congress Cataloging-in-Publication Data
Names: Felt, Christian, 1989– author.
Title: The lightning jar / by Christian Felt.
Description: Iowa City : University of Iowa Press, 2018. |
Series: The John Simmons Short Fiction Award |
Identifiers: LCCN 2018008669 (print) | LCCN 2018014227
    (ebook) | ISBN 978-1-60938-601-6 | ISBN 978-1-60938-600-9
    (pbk. : alk. paper)
Classification: LCC PS3606.E435 (ebook) | LCC PS3606.E435 L55
    2018 (print) | DDC 813/.6—dc23
LC record available at https://lccn.loc.gov/2018008669

To Carlin

Contents

The Lightning Jar

The Smallest Cousin

AMANDA KNEW the secrets of the Lake. She'd written most of them herself. "On the surface it may look blue," she said, "but underneath for miles and miles it is black. If you swam to the bottom, both your eyes and ears would pop. Down there, the water is heavier than solid rock."

"Does anything live there?" Karl asked, hugging his knees.

"Only fish with lamps on their heads."

"They sound pretty."

"Like stars but you don't fully understand. I wish I could describe how much they'd like to eat you!" Amanda clenched her fists.

"What do they eat in reality?" Karl asked.

"Each other, of course. There's no one else."

Mom's gong rang and the children's cardhouses fell in.

"That wasn't Mom's fault," Amanda said. "I shook the floor." She pounded the floor with her hands, then jumped from the loft onto her bed and ran downstairs.

"Today the soup is fish," Mom said, pretending she ran a one-table restaurant that served whatever she felt like at the moment. *The atmosphere is that of an ideal dinner en famille,* one critic had written.

Fortunately, he wasn't in attendance today.

Were the children…*sad*? Karl crushed his fish with a spoon. Amanda sighed. She sighed again and said, "When do our cousins get here? I'm bored."

A distant storm cleared its throat. Mom looked out the window and saw the purple instant when the waves disappear entirely before beginning to fan away from shore.

"Your cousins arrive on Friday," she said. "Enjoy your privacy while you can." *When they get here, then you'll be sorry. There'll be no more hiding in the loft, no more reading by the fire. Their voices will even drown out the rain on the roof.*

"Ooh!" Karl pointed. "Lightning."

"Turn your chair around so you can watch while you eat," Mom said. *Chez Maman* did not stand on ceremony.

The Cousins arrived on Friday, as forecast. Some were big and some were small, but none of them seemed quite human. They outnumbered the beds by ten to one, and at night their sleeping bags spangled the floor like cocoons. The smallest one slept under Karl's bed. Its sounds kept Karl awake, partly because he couldn't be sure whether or not he was just imagining them.

The next morning, the Cousins began assigning roles for *The Chronicles of Narnia* without asking Amanda, who stamped her foot and said, "Even though there are more of you and some of you are bigger than me, I am still in charge."

"How come?" the Cousins said.

"The first rule," Amanda said, "is that we don't waste nice sunny mornings playing inside."

"There'll be lots of sunny mornings," the Cousins said.

"No, there won't," Amanda said. "We have storms every day at the Lake."

"No one has storms every day."

"We do. It's in the Book. Wait here." Amanda returned with the Book and read: *"At the Lake, we have storms every day."*

Karl felt embarrassed. He thought the Book should have said something like, *Located at the bull's-eye of the Spiral Mountain Chain, the Lake swallows clouds like suds going down a drain . . .*

The Cousins looked skeptical.

"It's funny about me," Amanda said, clapping the Book shut, "but reading makes me want to joust. Who will be my horse? Karl, choose one, too, and we'll have a tournament."

The Cousins reared and whinnied. They enjoyed being ridden. Amanda chose an enormous white charger, while Karl picked a nag with a kind face. It seemed grateful to have been chosen, which was why Karl chose it, but—oh!—he'd rather be outside.

Karl enjoyed lightning even more than most people. He wondered if you could trap it by having it strike the lip of a jar at just the right angle so the electricity would spin around forever in a ball. What would you do with such a jar? Read by it, perhaps, but if you looked at it directly you'd go blind.

The storm that night was especially fierce. It sounded like chains sliding off the roof, and the lightning seemed to light up only the most frightening parts of Karl's room. The smallest Cousin whimpered with each thunderclap. Eventually, Karl climbed down to sit by it under the bed.

"Is it the thunder that worries you, or the lightning?" he asked.

"Both," the Cousin said. "But especially the lightning."

"That's sensible," Karl said. "Of the two, lightning might fry you up, while thunder isn't much more than a noise." Yet why pretend that noises couldn't hurt you? When Karl was younger, a creeping sound in the walls had made him eat his own hair. "Go get the Book," Karl said. "We'll see what it has to say about lightning."

"*In the average year*," Karl read, "*the Lake is struck ten thousand times, completely depriving the water of smell. No research has yet been undertaken on the contribution of electricity to the evolution of fish, but you only have to look at the Pale Headless Scruffy, for instance, to know that Something is going on . . .*"

Lightning flashed exactly as Karl turned off his flashlight, blurring his sense of cause and effect. Had lightning got into his own evolution, he wondered, in tiny pieces through the lungs? He moved to go, but the smallest Cousin grabbed his elbow.

"I'm not ready to be alone yet," it said, and Karl decided to share his secret.

"I have a theory that you could trap lightning in the right kind of jar. Would you feel better if you caught some lightning of your own?"

"Like a pet?" the Cousin asked.

"I suppose . . . You could name it and take it for a walk. But it wouldn't really care . . . On the whole, lightning is not like a dog. You can't bury your face in it."

"But would it growl? Would it eat birds?"

"*Birds?*" Karl laughed. "Let's consult the Book . . . *The mystery of lightning, deferred but not explained by science, is how it lives—as it must be said to live—on nothing, or even less: the distance between one body and another.*"

"I don't understand," the Cousin said.

"But do you feel better?" Karl yawned.

"I'm going to name mine Robert and feed it grass."

"Then I'll be getting back to bed," Karl said.

"What I'm *really* scared of," the Cousin said, holding onto his arm, "is spiders. You know how they sound at night, when they're not bothering to be sneaky anymore? It's the worst I know."

Karl sighed. "Come on, then." He lifted the Cousin into bed. It curled up by his feet and slept peacefully, while Karl stared at the ceiling, trying not to hear anything at all.

Before the others were awake, Karl laid out jars along the seawall. He blew the dust out of each one, hoping they were empty enough, and placed a carrot at both ends, as far apart as possible. "I know lightning doesn't like carrots *per se*," he muttered to an imaginary teacher. "That's not the point."

The smallest Cousin followed him, humming a tune. It was very irritating. "Why don't you go and wake your siblings up?" Karl said.

"They'd get angry. Besides, even if they asked me to play, I'd rather stay here with you."

"Oh." The Cousin had a crush. "You're going home tomorrow, right?" Karl said.

The Cousin toed a circle in the sand.

Karl began to explain about the jars. While he talked, the sky and Lake merged into a single band of grey. He guessed there was about an hour left before the storm.

If you asked Mom did she like the Cousins, she might say don't ask me while I'm doing their laundry. She washed their castoff shells, it seemed, every day, yet the Cousins always found something smudgy to wear. At the moment, they were rumbling at the top of the stairs, gathering. Mom turned off her Sibelius. What she missed most was silence. If only you could punish them, like Karl, simply by raising an eyebrow or asking an unkind question. You could shout at the Cousins, but it was no good trying to talk to them. You had to separate one from the pack, make it understand it wasn't in trouble, then listen as it referred to itself as we and answered questions with jokes.

Mom grabbed one of the Cousins as it rushed by.

"What subject do you enjoy most at school?" she asked. She was saving the good questions for when they had established rapport.

"Lunch!" the Cousin said and burst into laughter. It tried to leave but Mom held on.

"How are you liking it here?"

"Fine." It became suspicious. "What's wrong? Can't we go play?" The others gathered around the sofa, murmuring, and Mom began to feel scared.

"I'll let you get back to your game," she said, and the Cousins ran off, shouting and hitting each other.

Mom started putting away their blocks, then sat cross-legged on the floor and began to build a tower herself. It collapsed when a door slammed upstairs.

What were they doing in the bathroom that was so funny?

Mom felt old.

Karl peeked under Amanda's door, knowing it was wise to spy on a game before deciding whether or not to participate. This morning, it seemed Amanda had gotten into trouble with a gang of paper dolls.

"Why do you hate us?" one Cousin's doll asked Amanda's.

"Because you're stupid," Amanda's doll replied, turning warily as the others encircled her. "And ugly."

"What a nasty thing to say! But we'll forgive you if you marry Todd."

Amanda's doll thought about it. She was badly outnumbered. "Which one of you is Todd?" she asked. A naked Ken doll raised its hand.

"No," Amanda said. "I'd rather kill myself first." She tore her doll in half and tossed the pieces in the air. The Cousins cheered and fought over them.

Amanda struck Karl with the door as she came out. "Why are you sitting there?" she said. "Couldn't you see I needed help?"

"I'm sorry," Karl said.

"There's no need to apologize. I can take care of myself. Let's go talk to Mom."

She seemed angry but Karl could tell she wanted to cry. The Cousins had brought a piece of school with them to the Lake.

Mom was popping the ends off beans while the smallest Cousin sat on the edge of the table and made a rabbit with its hands, singing, "*There was a little house in the middle of the woods . . .*"

Karl stood with Amanda in the doorway, watching.

"Don't you know any other songs?" Mom asked.

"Just one," the Cousin said. "Would you like to hear it?"

"Please."

"*There was a little house in the middle of the woods . . .*"

"Are you sure they're not the same?" Mom asked.

"I know they sound the same so far," the Cousin said reassuringly, "but they may have a different ending."

Karl and Amanda went over and sat down. Karl looked at his mother in a defeated sort of way.

"Earlier," she said, "we were talking about how to improve the house so that we can all enjoy it here more together next summer. You had some excellent ideas," she said to the smallest Cousin. "Would you like to share them with Amanda and Karl?"

"Well," the Cousin said, "I thought maybe a slide from top to bottom of the house."

"Hmm," said Karl, who had suggested that years ago. "Wouldn't that be too expensive?"

"You had other ideas," Mom prompted.

"Oh, well, they're all too *expensive*, if you put it that way . . ." The Cousin blushed. "I thought the point was to make us happy."

Karl was looking out the window when lightning struck the beach. A purple birch tree faded from his eyes. A white roar filled his ears.

He ran outside to check the bottles. One had rolled off the seawall and shattered on the rocks. The others were full of rainwater that wasn't even fizzing, superheated, or purple.

How could you keep a jar open for lightning but at the same time prevent it from filling up with rain? The problem seemed insoluble ... unless, perhaps, plastic wrap?

"Come inside now, Karl," Mom said, walking up behind him. Apparently she didn't see how ridiculous it was to expect that lightning would strike the same place twice.

"The particles are depleted," Karl tried to explain. "We'll never be so lucky again."

She put her hand on his shoulder and guided him back toward the house.

"Maybe you just need a bigger jar," the smallest Cousin said comfortingly.

Mom tripped over something in the sand. Karl got down on all fours. "I've read about this," he said. "The lightning has turned the sand to glass."

A jagged, glassy tube—it might go down for miles! The lightning might still be trapped at the bottom.

"Don't touch!" he said, but it was too late. With a brave giggle, the smallest Cousin had leaped down the hole.

"What do we do?" Karl asked.

"Don't worry," Mom said. "He'll come back when he's ready. Anyway, his parents will never notice the difference."

"Just keep the hole free from sand," Amanda said.

"I'll put some food down there, too." Karl said. "What do Cousins eat?"

The Lightning's Ghost

THE COUSINS LEFT without noticing that any of them were missing, and Mom did not remind them. Whatever might happen to the smallest Cousin under the beach, it was better than growing up with its family. Each morning, Karl used a paper funnel to pour crumbs down the tube, which fortunately did not get clogged. One morning, he poured some grape juice down, too, but the jug was so heavy he ended up pouring more than he'd intended. Much more.

That night, Karl and Amanda were playing "Murder in the Dark" when Karl fell with his ear near the tube. He heard laughter. He looked down the tube and saw light. It flickered shyly and he recognized his smallest Cousin. "Get a jar," he told Amanda. "No," she said. He got a jar and placed it over the tube. The Cousin did not come up so he put his mouth over the tube and sucked. His lungs were too weak to bring up any grape juice, but with a puff the Cousin filled his throat. He spat it into his palm.

There were two of them! As soft as milkweed and impervious to spit, they immediately began to float away. He clapped the jar over them and screwed on the lid.

"Who's the other one?" Amanda said.

"The lightning," Karl said. His heart throbbed.

The children were pleased with their new ghosts but unsure what to do with them besides keep them a secret from Mom. She preferred people with interesting secrets. The ghosts were too faint to read by and disappeared entirely during the day. If you put your ear to the glass, you could hear the ringing which Karl had mistaken for laughter. But it was impossible to discern any words.

The next day, the children found an unexpected use for their ghosts. Amanda had become health-conscious ever since she'd read that heart failure felt like being sat on by a huge black dog. So she took Karl on a walk along the highway.

"Imagine how beautiful today's freeways will look as artifacts," she said, "half buried in sand or covered with moss and crocodiles!"

Karl was tired of hearing quotations from her Book. He scooped up a beetle and wondered if its mouth were too small for biting. The highway stretched for hundreds of miles in either direction, and strange insects, including Jerusalem Crickets, lived in the ditches on either side. It was entirely possible their eggs glommed on to passing cars.

A pair of Spanish tourists pulled up and asked in English, "Do you know the way to the nearest public beach?" They were handsome and Karl racked his brains for them, but he couldn't think of a single beach except the one by his house, which was private.

"There is no sand here that would not be polluted by your feet," Amanda said in her stilted Jämtish, which she referred to as "Local."

"What?" the Spaniards said.

"Go north," Karl translated. The Spaniards thanked him and drove on.

Returning home, Amanda and Karl found a pair of Knudsen children building a sand castle on their beach. Amanda introduced herself in Local, but the Knudsens pretended not to hear. If your accent wasn't just right, that's what Locals would sometimes do. They wore grey clothes that made Amanda feel ashamed of her tulip-yellow shorts.

So, she thought, real Lake people dress like it's winter all year round.

She couldn't think of anything to say, so she watched Karl show his beetle to the smaller Knudsen in ordinary Swedish.

"It's very beautiful," the smaller Knudsen replied. "Where did you get it?"

"We found it by the road," Karl said. "Feel free to stroke it."

"Then it could be from anywhere!"

"There's nowhere better than here," Amanda said.

The boys held their palms side by side so the beetle could cross. Amanda was afraid Karl would be flattered into showing the smaller Knudsen his ghost. But he left the bottle in his pocket. They didn't know the Knudsens quite well enough for *that*.

"We met some Tourists today," she said to the larger Knudsen. "Terrible people."

"How so?" the larger Knudsen asked.

Amanda struggled to find the Local words: "They were fat, noisy, smelly, and loud. They wanted to use our beach, but we scared them off."

"You should have directed them to our farm," the larger Knudsen said. "Mom's renting out rooms for the Cloudberry Festival, and they could have used our lovely beach."

If the Knudsens had such a lovely beach, then why were they here? Did they want to be friends?

"Ah yes, the Cloudberry Festival," Amanda said. "Our family has been celebrating that for generations."

"Mom invented it about ten years ago," the larger Knudsen said. "At first, it was just to squeeze money out of the Tourists, but now we all look forward to it. There's music, dancing, games. My brother and I dress up as Wisps, and everyone is encouraged to wear cloudberries on their fingers. Oh, it's fun!"

"Sounds nice," Amanda said, wondering how to get herself invited. "I hate everything sticky," she said. Then the smaller Knudsen began to laugh.

"Look, the beetle is king of the castle!" he said. The beetle scrabbled over the rampart and fell twenty thousand feet onto its back, kicking furiously.

The Doctor was a general practitioner and folklorist who didn't deserve his reputation among the Local children as a mad scientist or vampire.

"You have the house for it, though," Mom said.

"The hair, too," he said, "but my interest in dead bodies is purely academic. Are you familiar with the Local zombie myth?"

Mom was not.

"Well, zombie is a clumsy word. The Wisps are clever and swift. Sometimes they tell jokes, but mostly they just moon about like little moons and if you get too close they drag you underwater, if they were drowned as children, or pull you inside a tree, if as children they were lost in the woods."

"How confusing. It seems like the Locals ought to have invented not one monster but two."

The Doctor glanced out the window. "Sometimes I'm not sure they 'invented' any monsters at all . . . The Local word for drowning also means remorse, nostalgia, and suffocation. They say there are clearings in the woods where no air exists at all. There, the mushrooms grow to spectacular sizes and birds drop dead as they fly through. That's where the Wisps sing so beautifully you can't resist . . . Please have more cake; I only like it when it's stale."

"Thank you," Mom said. "You confused me with the word zombie.

I actually have heard of these Wisps. My children are planning to impersonate them during the Cloudberry Festival."

The Doctor frowned. "Have they been making Local friends?"

"The Knudsen children have been very kind. They offered us a live chicken. Was it very rude that I refused?"

"The Wisps are said to resemble foreigners," the Doctor mused, "though of course they were Local enough before they died . . . Don't worry, the Locals expect us to be rude. The ruder we are, the better they like it."

Karl was wandering through the forest behind the Doctor's house. White fungus speckled the pines. Crowberry vines twined their trunks with eyes. High up, a squirrel made a mournful sound, and down low, a mournful smell made Karl think: So many creatures live their whole lives underneath! What if, as an old man, I learned that a dragon had been living inside the Mountain all along? Would I have any memories that *didn't* change?

The sun made him look up. There was a clearing with a caravan and a brook. Children were wading. One of them wore a Stingrays cap, and the other had a monkey on her shoulder. They didn't seem to notice Karl, but their monkey did. The Stingrays cap was red. So was the Gypsy, sitting on the caravan, eating plums. He beckoned to Karl with his knife.

"Are you the Doctor's child?" he said.

"No, I'm Karl," Karl said, and immediately regretted having given his real name.

"Well, Karl, if you see the Doctor, tell him we are comfortable. Grandma should arrive tomorrow, and she will tell him everything."

"OK," Karl said. "Are you here for the Cloudberry Festival?"

"I *am* the Cloudberry Festival!" the Gypsy said, smiling redly. "My brothers and I have been hired to play our violins. Do you want to exchange gifts?" He looked at Karl appraisingly, and Karl realized the children were standing right behind him.

"What have you got in your pockets?" the girl asked.

Karl had toothpaste, mints, a plastic stegosaurus, and of course the jar with ghosts in it. He wanted to keep it a secret, but somehow the boy already had it in his hands and was turning it over in the sun. It sure *looked* empty.

"The toothpaste is for me," the Gypsy said. He unscrewed the cap and sniffed. "I love the smell."

The girl said, "Since there's nothing good, I'll take the mints. And the stegosaurus."

The Gypsy spoke to her sternly and she went into the caravan.

"Can I have this?" the boy asked, holding the jar. Karl was so flattered, he almost said yes. But he couldn't just give his smallest Cousin away.

"I'm sorry," he said, "but it's a family ghost."

"A ghost!" The boy looked at it more closely. "I was hoping it was that."

"Do you know much about ghosts?" Karl asked.

"Don't bother our guest," the Gypsy said, and the boy slunk into the caravan.

The girl came out and gave Karl a wooden flute shaped like an owl.

"Please accept our humble gift," she said. "You blow in the front, like this." She let him try. "It scares away demons," she added skeptically.

"Thank you," Karl said. The mouthpiece was damp.

"Now it's time for you to go," the Gypsy said. He was looking pretty angry or bored, so Karl went.

As the forest closed behind him, he regretted the poverty of his gifts. Perhaps coming from a foreigner, though, even a stegosaurus and toothpaste were special. Above all, he regretted not having had a present for the boy, who was able to get quite close before Karl heard him and spun around.

"Don't be scared," the boy said. "I wanted to give you this." He took off his cap and offered it to Karl.

"It's beautiful," Karl said. He shook out some dandruff before putting it on. "So are you going to help your father play for the Cloudberry Festival?"

"I'm so unmusical," the boy said, "I'm not even allowed to listen."

"So you're not coming?"

"I wish I could. I don't even know where the festival is. Dad doesn't want us getting to know the Locals."

"It's at the Knudsens' farm," Karl said. "Please come."

"I have to go," the boy said. But after a few steps, he turned around: "You have to drown your ghost."

"What?"

"Otherwise it will only bring you misery and discontent."

"It's my smallest cousin," Karl protested.

The boy smiled. "Your cousin is dead. I'm sorry." He ran away.

Karl took out his flute and played it. He pretended to be an owl, bobbing his head with each wingbeat, dodging trees at the last possible second. He could see the flashes of blood beating within his prey. He began to make up a beautiful tune. This game would never work without music, which melted so many imaginary obstacles.

But when he took his jar out, even in the darkest part of the forest, there still didn't seem to be anything there.

Machines crouched around the Knudsens' barn like sleeping dinosaurs. The threshing floor was covered with sawdust, and trestle tables were piled high with cloudberry pastries and preserves. The barnyard was floodlit for dancing, and Mrs. Knudsen stood by the punch bowl with an apron full of money, ready to sell fruit and make change.

Karl and Amanda had come early in order to hide before the Tourists arrived. Unsure how Wisps dressed, they'd just worn ordinary clothes and floured their faces. The key to their costumes, after all, was their ghosts, which hung around their necks. It had not been hard putting them in separate jars, since they floated so slowly. But Karl had been conscious of the danger should one of them drift away. The lightning's ghost, which Amanda carried, shone more brightly, but the smallest Cousin's somehow did more to catch the eye. Karl had to force himself to stop looking or else he began to feel dizzy and have thoughts that were not his own.

The Knudsens, bearing flashlights, were impressed.

"Those are amazing," the smaller Knudsen said. "How did you make them?"

"It's a secret," Amanda said. Karl had to agree.

He was going to ask what they should do if they managed to lure a Tourist away from the herd when the smaller Knudsen looked at his Stingrays cap and said, "That's mine."

"The Gypsies gave it to me," Karl said.

"Ah." The smaller Knudsen didn't seem particularly impressed. "They steal our scissors, too."

"Can you believe it?" the larger Knudsen said. "They stole so many, we couldn't make a banner for our own festival!"

"Time to go," the smaller Knudsen said as headlights swept the field. "Remember to stay in the deep grass."

"Make subtle noises and keep your light moving," the larger Knudsen said. "You never want to appear ordinary."

"No problem," Amanda said.

The Knudsens flitted away, blinking their flashlights. A bird crossed the moon, and the children's ghosts shone more brightly. Amanda took Karl's hand and said, "Let's stay together for a bit."

"OK," he said.

"Like lovers who have drowned in each other's arms."

"OK."

They wandered toward the forest.

"I just don't think it's probable . . ." Karl said, letting go of her hand.

"What?"

"Lovers drowning in each other's arms. There'd be too much struggle."

"Not if one knocked the other out first and held on to her like an anchor while she sank," Amanda said. She sounded almost angry about it.

Karl took out his flute and played the first part of "Good King Wenceslas." The forest hooted back, then struck up a violin. The Gypsies emerged, playing as they came. When they finished, the Tourists cheered. Some threw money. Mrs. Knudsen watched jealously where it fell. A small figure rushed out to gather the coins. Karl hoped it was the Gypsy boy, but it was just his monkey.

"You're not flitting," Amanda said.

"Sorry," Karl said.

Nobody seemed to be paying attention to them, so they flitted closer to the crowd. Somehow, Mrs. Knudsen had found time to complain about the Gypsies' thefts.

"What's the big deal about a few scissors?" one Tourist said.

"There's plenty for everyone," another said, paying fifty crowns per cloudberry.

"If we had Gypsies back in Milwaukee, I'd leave out scissors just for them."

"What a tune!"

"The music is good," Mrs. Knudsen said, "but the best parts are stolen from us. Listen, my husband is about to play the concertina. Now you'll hear real music."

Mr. Knudsen struck up a waltz. It was jolly enough, but couldn't match the excitement of the Gypsy band. Fortunately, the Gypsies decided to play along with him, and soon the dancing was wilder than before. The Tourists danced like people who ordinarily wouldn't even try—not *really*—which only increased Karl's pleasure in watching them laugh and flush, stumble over each other's feet and fall into each other's arms.

If only the boy had come!

"Do you want to dance?" he asked Amanda shyly.

"We have a job to do," she said.

But nobody had even noticed the Wisps. Karl felt like a raccoon peering into a dining room at night, watching people eat. The Book had said, "For you, being human is just a habit; but for me it's joy—a holiday." Karl thought he knew what it meant.

"I'm going to wash this flour off my face and dance with Mom," he said. But Amanda pulled him back into the grass. There was clearly much at stake for her in being a Wisp.

The Knudsen children were having an easier time. In their quaint costumes, they'd pull a Tourist aside and laugh him into buying something. Karl and Amanda hadn't even been given—or thought to bring—anything to sell.

Before long, the Knudsen children had joined the party outright, eating pancakes with their fingers and dancing with their friends.

Karl wondered if his ghost had made him hard to see. Sometimes, a Tourist would seem to look at him for a moment, as if remembering something sad. But in the end, the Tourist always looked away.

Toward midnight, Karl heard Mom asking where her children were.

"They were around here somewhere," the larger Knudsen said. "Maybe they've gone home?"

Mom stood with folded arms, scanning the grass. Karl raised his lantern in salute, but her eyes passed right through him.

His sorrow at being hidden from the world gradually turned into a strange kind of joy. Walking home, neither he nor Amanda spoke, as if afraid of breaking a spell. They didn't bother to brush their teeth and went to bed with flour on their faces, lanterns on their chests.

As Karl fell asleep, he seemed to hear the smallest Cousin speak: "You think we will be happier together, but I'm not happy, not happy, not..."

Nothing Happens

NOTHING HAPPENS, but we're happy, my sister and I. We weed the beach for money then walk to the gas station to spend it on firecrackers. We build mansions for beetles then blow them up. We rescue a swallow that has fallen out of its nest. It won't eat spinach, raisins, or ham. We bury it in the dog house that still doesn't seem empty after fifty dogless years. During storms, we run outside, tickled by the idea of our deaths falling from the sky. On sunny afternoons, we tell ghost stories in a closet and argue over which is scariest. We put on Mom's makeup and argue over who is prettiest. We never talk about the future—college or marriage or getting a job. Our biggest hope is that someday Mom will let us get a dog. We hunt many creatures but catch few of them. We have no friends except each other. We don't need any. There's always one more month, one more week, one more day before we have to leave. Even one more hour is time enough for nothing to happen, and as long as nothing happens, we have nothing to fear.

The Guest and the Gorbel

THE GUEST WAS only related by marriage. His real name was Olle. "Also, he smells like Cheerios," Amanda said.

"The cat likes him," Karl said.

"He bribes it," Amanda said. "When we're not looking, he feeds it things that rot its teeth."

"He only does that to be kind," Karl said.

The trouble was, the Guest didn't seem to have a very clear idea of what kindness looked like.

He arrived late in August when the prospect of going back to school was waking like a virus in the children's blood. He stood in the doorway, letting the mosquitoes in. He told them not to let him interrupt. But it was impossible to continue playing dead with the Guest watching. It was impossible to tell whether or not he approved. It didn't even cross Karl's mind to invite him to join in.

Even Amanda had to admit the Guest was more to be pitied than despised. "I hope I'd have problems if *my* mom died," she said.

"Shhh, he might be listening!" Karl said.

"Look what I found in the trash can while looking for gum." She handed Karl a piece of paper.

"#556," it read. "I hate you / You hate me / I flush the toilet / Bye-bye pee."

They took the poem to Mom.

"I don't think you have anything to worry about," she said. "It's perfectly normal for people your age to be interested in excrement."

"It's a question of degree," Amanda said.

Mom sighed. "I want each of you to find a way to cheer him up," she said. "Amanda, why don't you paint with him?"

"I'm not painting with someone who's traumatized. It isn't fair."

"You have advantages of your own," Mom said. "And Karl—perhaps he'd like to help you catch grasshoppers?"

"I don't know..."

"Just try *something*, alright?"

It took a while before Mom realized the Guest was watching her. She tried to continue doing her crossword puzzle, but all the joy was gone.

"Are you hungry?" she asked, turning around.

The Guest seemed to consider the question seriously without coming to a decision. Mom placed a gingersnap on the table just in case. The Guest sniffed it, then followed Mom to the sink and squatted in her shadow while she washed the dishes. No doubt he liked the smell of soap.

"So, how are you getting on?" Mom asked. She kept on washing even after all the dishes were clean, assuming the Guest would feel more comfortable if they were facing opposite directions and her hands were busy.

"There's a spider under my bed," he said.

"Oh. Have you asked Karl to look?"

"It always stays in the same place."

"Are you sure it's alive?"

"And looks at me. I don't know."

Mom took a deep breath. "So what do you want to do this summer? There's still a lot of time left before school. You could write a play, or build a fort, or paint a picture . . ."

"Yes, I will paint. I can clean up after myself," the Guest said defensively. "And don't let Karl kill my spider."

The cat followed him down the hall. Mom hoped it wouldn't get attached, since the Guest wasn't staying very long.

That afternoon, Karl saw a white bird on the berm. A child seemed to be molesting it, and Karl ran to help. But as he got closer, the bird turned into the Guest's watercolor pad, flapping in the wind. "It's impossible to work like this," the Guest said. The wind pulled a blue drop off his brush and flung it across his face. He spluttered and let go. The painting was torn off his pad and landed on the water. It bobbed, colors sifting together.

"How dumb," the Guest said.

"Well, you chose a windy spot," Karl said cautiously. "Why don't you paint indoors?"

"I can't paint when other people are watching."

Karl looked away. "I thought your painting was really good," he said. "Everyone says you're talented."

The Guest grunted. "I wanted to go out on the boat," he said. "But you don't have one."

"We used to," Karl said helpfully.

But the Guest wasn't interested.

"Where's Amanda?" he said. "Is she hiding from me?"

"Yes," Karl said. He couldn't bring himself to lie. "But she promised to do something with you later."

"Let's go find her," the Guest said, and gathered up his things.

. . .

From Amanda's window, the Guest looked just like a smudge of colored chalk.

Amanda's door was closed and dark beneath. Karl laid his cheek on the carpet, looking across its hills of red and pepper green.

"Tell her I'll be waiting in my room," the Guest whispered, suddenly shy, and crept off down the hall.

Karl knocked.

"Who is it?" Amanda said in a high voice.

"Just Karl."

Amanda cracked the door. "Funny weather we're having," she said.

"He wants you to play with him," Karl said.

"Oh." Amanda let him in. She fell backward on her bed. "But I don't want to play with *him*. It's not that I'm mean, really. I just don't know how."

Karl sat beside her. "Choose a board game," he suggested. "It doesn't have to be fun."

Amanda seemed to consider. "Well, I do have an idea—if you promise not to tell Mom."

"I promise. All she wants is for the Guest to be happy."

Amanda smiled.

She propped the blanket over their heads with an old rifle and shined the flashlight up her face. Perhaps the effect was childish, but it was too late to take it back now.

The Guest's expression was as unreadable as a dish of snow.

"This is the story of Grandma Susan," Amanda began, "an old woman who lived alone and grew vegetables by the Lake. Her children were far too busy with their careers to ever come and visit her, so she was always alone, except for her cat, which was where the trouble started.

"To understand this story, you must realize that tomatoes usually grow on bushes and are round or lumpy, but not in any particular way.

So Grandma Susan was surprised one morning to find a huge tomato growing in the soil like a beet. She dug it up and washed it off. The top was red and shiny, but the bottom was gross and spongy, with the face of Susan's youngest daughter Nicole on it.

"She slapped it and whispered *Nicole*, but it didn't respond. She really loved Nicole. That afternoon, Grandma Susan got a phone call that said Nicole had been killed in a knife accident so naturally she couldn't bring herself to cut the tomato up, even though it was perfectly ripe and smelled delicious.

"So she left it on the table. It was nice having something besides her cat to talk to, even though the tomato didn't answer back. Every day it got redder and redder, and every morning Grandma Susan would squidge up its eyelids to make sure its beautiful blue eyes were still fresh. But one day, its eyelids tore and the seeds spilled out and Grandma Susan knew the time had come to decide."

There were so many possibilities! A murderer might break in and hang Grandma Susan's cat. The tomato might bite off Grandma Susan's fingers, or blast her with jets of boiling blood. She might discover an egg inside the tomato, containing the most poisonous spider in the world; a single bite would turn you into wood . . .

But the Guest was looking at Amanda so openly, almost as if he were a whole new boy. Now that she had him in her power, she felt merciful and said, "So Grandma Susan cut the tomato in two. She melted one half in a delightful red sauce, which she shared with her cat, George. That was the cat's name. The other half she buried in the garden where, next summer, a huge tomato bush grew up from the seeds. The tomatoes were blue, like Nicole's eyes, and whenever she fed them to her cat, it learned how to talk and never died. It told her many wonderful stories, which were a great comfort to Grandma Susan as she got older. The End."

On the whole, Amanda was pleased. It was hard to find an ending that was both happy and believable.

"That's not how the story ends," the Guest said.

"What?" Amanda said.

"George should never have drunk Nicole's sauce," the Guest said. "That was a big mistake. It was OK for Grandma Susan to drink Nicole's sauce because she was her mother. But the cat George was not immune. As he lapped up the delicious sauce, he felt something hairy creeping down his throat. Before he knew it, he wasn't George anymore. He had become a Gorbel, which is like a cat but also like a spider, and has no mouth except when it's eating and no eyes except when it's looking at something nasty. In fact, it doesn't exist at all unless it is up to some mischief or other.

"Grandma Susan didn't notice the change at first because even though she'd lived with George for twenty years, she'd never really gotten to know him. Yes, she had talked to him, but she had also talked to tomatoes. She wasn't picky. She'd never really noticed that George didn't listen, or that the Gorbel did.

"Listening to Grandma Susan, the Gorbel learned how to take pills and answer the telephone. It became an excellent cook. Unfortunately, it didn't find a purpose in life before it got hungry for more Nicole sauce.

"The Gorbel loved to eat Grandma Susan's tomatoes. But whenever Grandma Susan caught it stealing from her garden, she would hit it with her broom, which made it hiss and grow a little cleverer each time. Soon, it was too clever to get caught.

"The Gorbel hated Grandma Susan's broom. One day, it burned it with gasoline. But in its wicked way, it liked Grandma Susan. It liked Grandma Susan because she stroked it and fed it and talked to it, but above all, it liked Grandma Susan because she smelled like Nicole. There was Nicole sauce flowing through her veins. The Gorbel would sit at the foot of her bed, watching her sleep, and think: *If I ate her all at once, there would be no more Nicole sauce forever.* So it divided Grandma Susan into halves and melted one half in a delightful red sauce, and buried the other half in the garden, where next summer there grew—"

"Hush!" Amanda said. "Even if your mother is dead, that's no excuse. Even if she was killed right before your very eyes!"

"I'm sorry," the Guest said, looking confused. "I thought you wanted that kind of story . . ." He put his hand on Amanda's shoulder but she shrugged it off.

Crawling out of the tent, he dislodged the rifle, and the blanket came down on her head. She heard him run away, and thought about chasing him for a while.

But she decided to stay under the blanket instead.

Notes from the Bottom Drawer

AFTER THE GUEST left, Karl could see nothing between himself and the end of the summer. "Make a list of everything you don't want to forget about the Lake," Mom suggested. "You can keep it in your backpack and read it when you feel particularly awful."

Instead, Karl went through the house, opening all the drawers. Mom's clothes, the croquet set, the broken concertina—everything important was in its place. In Amanda's room he even opened the drawer he had never opened before, because Amanda said it contained the most poisonous spider in the world. But all Karl found was a typewriter, a resin nativity set, some Dala horses, and a large matchbox, which he slid open *very* slowly. But there were just some scraps of paper inside, with handwriting on them. Karl spread them out on the kitchen table where

Mom did her crosswords and tried to arrange them in a logical order:

> never been to the chicken
> Please remember milk
> I forgot your visa in the box
> when it struck me, you meant wire
> left me his knife as a useful
> contents undisclosed, but it's foreign
> here about the radiator, call 311
> peaches will be bad by Sunday
> if you bring illegal seeds
> By the time you read this I'll be
> sorry for the mess, I had to

Sounds sinister, he thought.

"That's Uncle Jonas' writing," Mom said. "I always envied him for getting to stay here in the winter with Grandma after we'd all gone home."

"Who's Uncle Jonas?" Karl asked.

Mom laughed.

"He was *my* uncle, not yours. An odd type, never married, never worked. We didn't talk about him if we could help it. I suppose we were ashamed . . . Funny to think how little that matters now!"

Karl gathered up the papers. "I'm going outside," he said stiffly.

The story of Uncle Jonas had wounded him deeply. The only alternative to ordinary life, it seemed, was shame—or death. Karl remembered how he'd felt when he first learned his body wasn't really his, only just for now.

"Only just for now"—he repeated the phrase until it sounded like a concentration camp.

He found the smaller Knudsen in the hammock and joined him for a nap.

When they woke up, he said, "What do you think of these?"

The smaller Knudsen read the notes slowly, drifting through the shade.

"Are they a to-do list or an apology?" Karl asked. "Or both?"

"Well . . . I'd say they have an unhappy ending," the smaller Knudsen said.

Karl reread the notes, frowning so hard it hurt. Then he lay back and looked at the sky.

"You know this is actually my hammock?" he said. "Even when I'm gone?"

"I never sleep in it then," the smaller Knudsen said.

Amanda pretended to nap for about ten seconds before jumping up to smack the wall. The creature inside skittered until she couldn't tell where it was, then stopped.

She'd seen its face among her books. It was probably just a mouse, but she couldn't sleep until she knew for sure. She couldn't let it stay here all winter by itself. She propped a cup over a pretzel. Now, if the creature ate the pretzel, the cup would fall and trap it.

Amanda pressed her hands against her head. There was something she'd forgotten to accomplish all summer, and now she couldn't remember what it was. She sorted her paper dolls according to beauty. But that wasn't it. She searched her drawers for treasure, but found only what she'd hidden there herself. Finally, getting hungry, she ate the pretzel and went outside.

"Karl!" she shouted. "*Karl!*" He was never around when you needed him. His hammock, empty, swung in the breeze.

Suddenly, she missed the Guest.

She didn't notice the cat at first because it was the same colors as the lilac bush. "You're awfully small for someone who spends so much time in the sun," she said. The cat accepted her caresses for a while, then ran.

"Cat, where are you?" she shouted. "*Cat!*" She thought about making a cat trap. But first she'd need a mouse . . .

Then she caught sight of it, licking itself on top of the fence inside the yellow rose bush.

There was no way to get in there without pain. "I love you," Amanda said grimly, and began to make her way.

But just as she came within grabbing distance, the cat sailed over her head and ran up the driveway. Amanda tore herself out of the bush and chased the cat onto the highway. She saw it vanish under the wheels of a car.

Its body lay in the cowpath on the other side of the road. Amanda's legs seemed to have turned to ice. But as she drew near, she found the cat was just relaxing. It had slipped to safety like a fish from between the paws of a cartoon bear. She stroked its belly. It flared its claws. She wondered where it would live all winter.

"I'd never be allowed to take you home," she explained. "I'll say goodbye now, just in case I don't get to see you tomorrow. We're leaving very early. If you get hungry, you might as well have a look around the house. But be careful; we leave out poison."

Mom held another match under the kindling and watched it die. The air up here was just too thin. Grandma Astrid had spent the last three years of her life on an oxygen tank. And rain had gotten into the woodpile. Leaks kept popping up, as if the house were being eaten. If Mom had termites, she would name them Hansel and Gretel. With an air of sacrifice, she fed her remaining crossword puzzles to the flame. There was no point in saving them for next summer when next summer might never happen.

Amanda came down the stairs, a blanket around her shoulders. "Have you enjoyed your last day?" Mom asked.

"I wish you wouldn't say 'last' in that condescending way."

"This fire is intended to cheer you up."

"I've forgotten something important," Amanda said. "It was supposed to make me very happy."

"It's too late now," Mom said. "Have you seen Karl?"

"No."

"Go get him, OK? It's our last evening together."

"That word again!"

In the long run, Mom believed it was kinder not to spare her children's feelings. They'd just have to harden, like everything else.

Amanda pulled her jacket over her head and ran into the pines. "Is Eskild still here?" she asked. That was the smaller Knudsen's name.

Karl felt around in the hammock. "He must have said goodbye while I was sleeping."

Amanda climbed in beside him. "I guess we won't see him again until next year."

"Do the Knudsens have school up here?" Karl asked.

"I don't even want to think about it," Amanda said.

They swung slowly back and forth. The rain puffed through the pines, misting their faces.

"We have to go," Amanda said.

"Have you heard of Uncle Jonas, who stayed here all year round?" Karl tried to sound casual.

Amanda stared. "Didn't he have a job?"

"He just lived here with Grandma Astrid, buying groceries and doing odd jobs and things. He never got married, and he read a lot ... I think he tried to be a writer."

"How could Mom not tell us?" Amanda said.

"Maybe she thought he'd set a bad example."

Amanda blew the skin off the coals. The smoke stung her eyes, giving her an acceptable reason to cry.

Karl was resting his head in Mom's lap. He seemed to need to talk, but when he spoke it was almost inaudible—a baby voice: "What happens to the house when we're gone? It just sits here, of course ... But it's never quite the same when we come back. *We're* never quite the same."

"Careful," Mom said, as a coal tumbled onto the rug. Amanda kicked it back into the fire.

"I like to imagine the whole house going up in flames," Karl said.

"We leave it in a smoking heap. Then next June, it's grown back fresh and green. The best part is, it didn't even exist during the winter while we were gone. There was nothing here at all . . ."

Amanda let her hair dangle close to the flames. They sounded like small jaws munching. So did the rain.

And there was the creature, winking at her from the mantel. She didn't mention it to the others. She never had. Perhaps it was just firelight on the beer steins, and if she looked carefully, it would disappear.

She closed her eyes tightly in order not to find out.

Snow on Snow

ONLY ONE ancient Greek composition survives in its entirety: the so-called Seikilos epitaph. Etched on a gravestone near Ephesus in the second century BC, it records a still-conventional commentary on death: "While you live, shine / have no grief at all / life exists only for a short while / and time demands its toll."

The sounds of the words and their musical accompaniment, which in Greek theory formed one inseparable whole, were probably more important than their sense. Unfortunately, these sounds are lost forever. Greek music notation, like our own, was not designed to represent sounds so much as the ideas behind them—melodies, harmonies, rhythms—using a closed system of symbols that makes sense only if you already know what the symbols refer to.

. . .

My father was born in Nash, Utah, in 1955, the only biological child of parents already in their thirties. His adopted sister, Karen, whom I've never met, left home early and now runs a bowling alley in Pocatello. At least, that's what she was doing the last time Dad mentioned her. Every Christmas, he sends her proteas from his hothouse—one of his quiet hobbies—each flower like a stuffed bird, wrapped in brown paper, with a card that reads simply, "xoxo."

Dad's father, a family-practice doctor, had been quiet in a way that inspired confidence in his patients. I never heard him say anything smart, but I never heard him say anything stupid, either, which probably counts for more. I'm not sure he had friends, really, but he had "golf buddies," "symphony buddies," family, dogs . . . Lots of people cried at his funeral, in the quietly straightforward way Mormons allow themselves in church.

I never feel much at funerals, as if there's anesthetic in the air. As long as I didn't look at the body, Grandpa still seemed alive, exerting his quiet fascination on a room. As people leaned over his casket to say goodbye, he seemed to be listening more carefully than ever.

Don't be fooled by the words: *diatonikos, harmoniai,* and *tonoi* may look familiar, but their referents are long gone. For instance, in Plato's *Republic, harmoniai* have nothing to do with the arrangement of simultaneous tones; rather, they refer to a mysterious totality of scale, rhythm, and textual subject which had a specific effect on moral character. The Mixolydian harmony caused grief and anxiety, while the Phrygian led to erotic ecstasy. Only the Dorian, fostering moderation and firmness, was permissible in the perfect city.

In old photos, Dad's mom, Laura, looks a lot like me. Perhaps we both just look a little overexposed. We share a lot of interests, too. There's a drawer at our house full of her stories, paintings, and illustrated compositions for piano: twelve-tone things, as well as Americana like "The Bride of Hiawatha," written, unsurprisingly, in trochees.

Her grandfather, John Moses Browning, had invented most of the guns produced by the Fabrique Nationale d'Herstal for World War I, which meant she had plenty of money. She went to Juilliard with the intention of becoming a concert pianist, but later switched to painting when she began to exhibit the symptoms of a rheumatoid arthritis that would prevent her holding a brush by the age of thirty, and kill her before she turned forty-five. It's hard to say if such a disease worked too fast or too slow.

She was forty-four when Dad, still a teenager, was called by the Mormon church on a two-year mission to Sweden. He wasn't particularly devout and had no knowledge of Swedish, but the General Authorities often issued such calls, it seemed, based less on one's personal qualities than on the qualities one's ancestors had possessed. And Dad's great-great-grandparents had been exceptionally zealous Swedes, pioneers to Utah in the days of ox and handcart, plural marriage and the Alphabet of Deseret, an attempt at phonetic spelling reform in which every symbol has just one sound.

The idea was to make writing easy—let everyone write the way they speak. But it never really caught on.

Plato's understanding of *harmoniai* derives from earlier writers' use of the word simply to refer to the way Greeks played music in different provinces: Lydia, Doria, Aeolia, Ionia, etc. Each people spoke a different dialect, and their speech gave rise to a different kind of melody, which in turn generated a different moral effect.

The same words—Lydian, Dorian, Aeolian—were reused for medieval church modes. But in the meantime, the music underneath them had changed. Instead of erotic ecstasy, for instance, the Phrygian now led to penitence and tears.

During the last decade of her life, Laura rarely left her room, whose excessive mirrors would have allowed no detail of her decline to go unnoticed. Sitting in the middle of the huge bed she and Grandpa used to share, she turned to an art form that was still accessible to her: writing. Sometimes, she fumbled with a typewriter; more often, she'd dictate to Dad, a sober schoolboy with few friends to keep him from his mother's side. When she grew tired of her own projects, she'd do Dad's homework. She dictated essays on science, literature, and history which earned him top marks, though she sometimes fudged a name or date, as if the encyclopedia had proved too cumbersome to handle. Her retellings of history give the sense of imagination at play:

"Do you think the Mexicans can overcome these palisades?" the youthful William Travis, hardly more than a boy, asked. One saw him manfully suppress the tremor in his chin.

Colonel Bowie laid a virile hand upon his shoulder.

"Never, my lad, as long as the Stars and Stripes do fly!"

The only subject Laura didn't do for Dad was math, which was probably why he got so good at it.

Dad brags about his mother's cheating—the only story I can remember him telling about her more than once—partly in order to shock, as an example of good-old-fashioned parenting that did no harm, but in a subtler way, I think, in order to prove he was loved as a child, to mitigate the slightly tragic aura that has surrounded his childhood. To this end, it doesn't really work.

Sometimes I imagine Dad as a puppet who has lost his ventriloquist. Every time he intends to say something beautiful—"I love you," for instance—his mouth stays shut. He listens for the words, but they just don't come.

Laura's drawer contains two unfinished plays, countless poems, some nude drawings, and the beginnings of thirteen novels. Her specialty, however, was the short story, typically about class conflict and the courage of young women whose naiveté is shattered by disaster: lovers dead in The War, fathers bankrupted by The Depression, legs paralyzed after Tragic Horseback Riding Accidents. She submitted a few of her stories to *Harper's* and the *Atlantic Monthly*; none of them were published. But she kept the rejection letters, with their polite critiques, as if planning to use them for future revision.

Though their notation survives only in scraps, the Greeks left behind a vast library of music theory. Philolaus, Pythagoras, Archytas, Aristoxenus, and others break down the scale—and the cosmos—into exact numerical ratios. Unfortunately, all their ratios are different. Philolaus' octave consists of five intervals of 9:8 and two of 256:243. Pythagoras' simple stack of fifths, each plucked from a string 3/2 the length of the last, unfortunately fails in its eleventh iteration to return to the starting note—preparing a chaos for Renaissance tuning and transposition that would not be resolved until the time of J. S. Bach's *Well-Tempered Clavier*.

Archytas' tunings, divided arbitrarily into enharmonic, chromatic, and diatonic forms, have no elegant mathematical basis, and are therefore thought to reflect actual Greek practice most closely.

Dad spent the first part of his mission in Östersund. He met my mom, Ida, while "tracting" door-to-door. She lived with her parents at the time, giving piano lessons in their living room and taking courses in English and modern languages at the local branch of Lund University. She was several years older than Dad, and almost as tall, with long black hair that she wore down her back in an intentionally archaic braid.

Now I'm going to do something odd and imagine my parents' first meeting, from Mom's point-of-view, in an overtly romantic way:

It's a dark afternoon, a few days before Christmas, and Ida's parents are out. She's curled up on the sofa, reading *Great Expectations* for the first time, when she hears a knock at the door. She rushes to open it, hoping for carolers—charming Swedish treats are waiting for them on a tray—but she finds a tall boy instead, like a bear stuffed into a suit. He stamps the snow off his shoes. From his collar rises steam. Instead of beginning to sing, he asks her in oddly formal Swedish, as if reciting from memory, if she believes in Christ, if she has heard of the Book of Mormon, if she is interested in finding out there is more to life than she's ever imagined.

"You'd better come in," she says.

She offers to take his coat, but he keeps it on. She gives him a charming Swedish treat, but he doesn't eat it. His hair is covered with snow that needs brushing off, but he just lets it melt. She offers him a seat on the sofa. He takes the chair opposite, staring mutely at the carpet, as if trying to remember his lines. She asks him what he has to tell her—what is so important?

He begins to speak very fast.

He says the angel Gabriel appeared to the teenage prophet Joseph Smith in Palmyra, New York, in the 1820s and showed the boy where to dig to find a set of gold plates containing a record of Christ's ministry in ancient America. Smith translated the plates, first by looking through miraculous crystal spectacles called the Urim and Thummim, later by dictating to a scribe while gazing into the darkness inside an ordinary top hat.

"And now I have his book to give to you." Dad uses the formal pronoun *er*, as though Ida is old. She feels old around him, in a protective way. She has trouble not laughing, watching him struggle with his briefcase. This must be almost his first time opening it. The snow drips off his coat. His face turns red.

"Let me," Ida says, taking the briefcase onto her lap. She's clever with such things. A few intuitive squeezes, and the lock springs open. She lifts out a book with a floppy leatherette cover and gilt lettering: *Mormons bok.* It's thinner than she expected. She bends it back and forth, dissatisfied. "I'd rather read the original," she says.

But the original, Dad explains, was written in Reformed Egyptian, the lingua franca of ancient America—a dead language like Latin even when the scribe Moroni used it to compile the gold plates. After Joseph Smith finished translating it, the original was taken by the angel Gabriel straight back to heaven.

"I mean *English*," Ida says, switching languages. Now she can't restrain her laughter. "We can talk English if you want." She holds up *Great Expectations* as proof.

"OK," Dad says.

Silence falls.

"What is your favorite music?" Ida asks.

After crossing the language barrier, they've found themselves in the no-man's-land of a first date.

Dad frowns as if she has posed him an existential puzzler.

"Beethoven . . . ?" It's probably the only composer he can think of.

Ida rushes to the piano and launches into a showy section of the "Hammerklavier" sonata. Most people would have stopped after making a few of Beethoven's major points, but Ida ploughs through all the way to the end of the movement.

Afterward, of course, she feels vulnerable—a little silly, slightly sublime. She knows Dad is standing behind her and waits for him to say something before she turns around.

In English, perhaps, he thinks, "That was embarrassing." But in Swedish, he says, *Vad vackert*: "How beautiful."

During my music theory classes in college, we spent a lot of time analyzing melody. But, strangely, we never addressed the fact that most of our terms were metaphors borrowed from other fields, as though melody were some kind of dark matter that could be observed only through its effects on surrounding space. We drew melodies on the chalkboard to show their "line," "shape," and "symmetry." We calculated their intervals and inferred their underlying harmonies like the unknown quantities in an equation. We referred to "motion," stepwise or by leaps, as though melody were a body, dancing across the harp inside the instructor's piano.

The instructor's hands, too, were dancers—hairy, five-legged men with flat pink hooves and gold thigh-rings, their movements far more primal than the two-part fugue they helped produce. Really, he had nice hands.

After her parents banned the missionaries from their home, Mom had to arrange meetings with Dad in cafés or other members' houses. She felt like she'd joined a communist cell, which at the time seemed like the right thing to do. With the arrival of spring, she started taking walks with Dad along the dirt road north of town as far as the ruins at Kronby: a leafy, laky, impossibly romantic prospect until the mosquitoes hatch.

Of course, Dad's mission companion was with him most of the time. He was even there during the First Discussion. I've left him out for narrative economy, but in fact his presence must have helped the courtship, lightening the burden of conversation for Dad, while preventing any irreligious display of affection from Mom that might have scared him off.

She realized the only way to continue seeing Dad was to continue receiving the discussions. She began attending church, accepted the "calling" of branch pianist, and read the Book of Mormon several times, finding it much better than she'd expected, possibly because her English was not as good as she liked to think.

She put off her baptism too long for Dad to do it. She wanted her parents' permission, and getting that took another year and a half, Grandma Astrid being against every change until it seemed inevitable.

In retrospect, parental resistance, like the chaperoning influence of Dad's companion, seems to have been well calculated to foster Mom and Dad's interest in each other for the long term. I wonder what kind of person, if any, Dad would have married had he not been transplanted into such propitious circumstances—the most fortunate of which was undoubtedly the language barrier.

Mom quickly discovered that the only way to have a conversation with Dad was in Swedish. He couldn't even read the discussions out loud in English without mumbling and blushing. For him, perhaps, English had grown too transparent to work as a means of personal expression. There was nothing left to hide behind. In Swedish, he could always blame a grammatical problem or mistaken word if he said something stupid, personal, or revealing. He could experiment with a new personality, one that was not ashamed of saying Unnecessary Things. In Swedish I have been, at times, his *älskling, ynkling, småkryp, kyckling, ädelsten, lille djur . . .*

One afternoon, shortly before we moved to Utah, I was daydreaming in the window seat when Dad came up and ran his fingers through my hair.

"*Är du ledsen, min gosse?* Are you sad, my boy?"

"Yes," I said, and he seemed to approve. We held our poses for a long time.

Only years later did it occur to me that Dad might be talking about his own sadness, rather than mine.

A mission was obligatory for young men of Dad's background; Mom was actually much more interested in religion than he was, and claims it was she who converted him to Mormonism during the course of long conversations in which she also taught him colloquial Swedish, discovered she was his fourth cousin, and comforted him when the letter arrived announcing his mother's death.

The letter, from Grandpa, contained only two sentences. When he showed it to Mom, she was astonished by its tone. She can't remember the exact words, which is unfortunate, because the exact words always matter, especially when there are so few of them.

After Dad returned home, he wrote Mom long letters. She says they were really good. Each one took a couple of weeks to cross the ocean, establishing a pleasant rhythm of suspense and relief. He proposed marriage and was accepted in written form, though it would take him another four years to finish his master's degree and get accepted to graduate school in Sweden.

In the meantime, he continued to write.

"He wrote you *letters*?" I ask Mom, my surprise falling on the plural. We're sitting on her bed in Laura's old room one evening during Christmas break. I've heard about the letters before, of course—I've even found the shoebox where they're hidden, cleverly, among shoes. But it's the kind of story that bears repeating, both to flatter Mom and to remind us who Dad used to be.

She goes into her closet and returns with the shoebox, turning it out dramatically on the bed.

I feign surprise.

"They're all in Swedish, of course," she says.

I start to open one but Mom takes it away: "I'd better find one that won't embarrass him too much . . ."

"Good luck with that."

Like Mom, I prefer to read books in their original language. Translation is made of analogy, and analogy can be stretched only so far before it snaps—or worse, goes limp.

Attempting to translate ancient rhythm, scholars assume that Greek music, like most living folk music, was based on repeating patterns of beats derived from the stresses of the spoken language. Even for thorough Greek theorists, rhythm went without saying because it was always being said.

Such analogies, while useful on the whole, iron out the irregularities, like subtle curves in the Parthenon, which must have held much of Greek music's meaning and beauty. The problem is the same one facing scholars who try to reconstruct Elizabethan pronunciation by assuming that all Shakespeare's end rhymes were full. Thus, *love* is made to rhyme with *prove*, although either may have sounded like *stove*.

The Whale Tax

DAD WAS DOING his crossword puzzle on the verandah, and Mons was just waking up from a nap he was taking inside a cardboard box for reasons he couldn't quite remember, but assumed were related to his sister, when a policeman began pounding on the door.

"Census!" the policeman said at regular intervals, but not as though he really cared. For a long time, Dad pretended to be gone but eventually it was impossible to do a crossword puzzle under the circumstances. So he turned Mons' box over on top of him and said, "Pretend you're a table."

Throughout the census, Mons was so table-like, he couldn't even hear what was being said. He heard only the wind in the pines, and without even knowing the word for it, he managed to imagine snow.

Dad lifted the box off his head and said, "I've told the policeman you're dead, so now the Morra will be less likely to eat you."

"I wish you hadn't . . ." Mons said, blushing.

His reason sounded like two forests being rubbed together. Did the Morra feel specially about him, or was she unable to tell the difference between him and empty space? She ate without looking, and never blinked with both eyes at the same time! He only hoped she wouldn't be scared if she ran into him in the woods, now, thinking he was a ghost.

Dad adjusted his wedding ring, a flower he picked every day (today it was white) and said, "As usual, My Future, I will get nowhere by talking with you. Here are fifty crowns and don't come back until dinner."

"I love you," Mons said quietly, looking out the window, where the sun was oozing through the fingers of the trees. The wind had blown the fig leaves off the statues again. *Poor Sister Phyllis will have a hard time walking home.* It was getting dark so early these days, perhaps she wouldn't even notice. Already, it was hard to tell his boat, drifting on the pond, from the reflection of a stone.

Mons kissed his father's unnaturally smooth chin, took his money, and left.

Of course, having *some* money only made him want more. Not for himself but for the Morra, who loved gold and jewels, or at least had some reason for preferring them to belong to herself.

One night—so misty, true, Mons might have mistaken a fish leaping out of the water for almost anything—he *believed* he had seen her huddling "round her warmthless fire." For a second, the sight had made even Mons turn away, susceptible to the legend that a direct glance from the Morra would turn a person into glass. She quite liked glass.

He took the bus into Drømö and spent half an hour in the jewelry shop trying to decide between seven things he couldn't afford. But Mr. Yllén gave him a discount because he liked Mons' face. People often pitied Mons despite the fact his home was a place, for instance, where people so rarely mentioned his deformity, he often forgot it even existed.

He bought a subtle topaz and dropped it on his way out of the shop.

Searching the sidewalk on his knees, Mons was distracted by the glitter of his own tears. But the stone itself had melted away.

Walking home with no money for the bus, Mons heard the pine needles like ribs under his feet. He considered calling off his treasure hunt, then saw a kingfisher cross the sun. What a world of riches there must be beneath the sea!

He rowed out his glass-bottomed coracle to perform a census. He intended to tax the aquatic creatures only in exchange for counting their dead.

First, he found a turtle chasing a pink jelly. It pumped in all the wrong directions and was soon caught and torn in half. Jellies seemed eager to avoid being eaten, but that was just a biochemical illusion. If they felt "pain," it didn't mean the same thing as for you or me. Not the same thing at all. "One Small Pink Jelly," Mons wrote on his clipboard, then crossed it out.

"How many of you are there, turtle?" he shouted into the water. A mosquito landed on his ear, but he let it stay.

The turtle finished swallowing. It stared at Mons inscrutably.

"Can I please have some treasure, just if you're not using it?" Mons put his hand in the water. To his surprise, the turtle swam up and flipped some jelly onto his palm.

Underwater, the jelly had rippled like cloth, but in the air it stood and wept prickly tears.

The mosquito took a sip and flew away.

"Watch out for . . ." it whined.

"I couldn't hear the last part of what you said," Mons said.

He hoped for better luck with the Pricklers, a tribe of industrious urchins who had settled the cliffs last January, driving off the unsavory Morays. Pricklers were known to scavenge shipwrecks and loved everything that glimmered. They spoke well but their voices were so small, they had to prepare their statements in advance and shout them in a chorus. It sounded impressive, but you could never tell what they were really feeling.

"How many Pricklers are you this year?" Mons asked.

After a burbling consultation they responded, *We are ninety-six. We lost seven to an acid wave last week. They were Sparkle-Quill, Quilliam and Spikeabelle, Dolores and Points-William, the Little Pricker and his brother Plush.*" Mons had trouble keeping track of all the foreign names and worried he had gotten some of them wrong as he drew a black line through the entire list.

"Well," he said sympathetically, "since you have lost so many loved ones you will not have to pay so many taxes."

The Pricklers whispered among themselves.

"*Taxes?*" they said.

"Shiny-shiny just for me," Mons said, feeling a little patronizing. "Just if you happen to have any ..."

With fish scales on its quills, one young Prickler was able to swim up and land in Mons' hand. It kissed his palm in a prickly sort of way, then rolled off, leaving behind a sapphire the size of a robin's egg.

Mons held the stone up to the sky. It seemed to pour the sky onto his face. But as it dried, the jewel turned grey from the inside out, frosting over with salt. Mons spat on it, rubbed it with jelly, but nothing would do. Only immersing it in the water returned its true color.

Despite its blueness, it felt warm. He decided to keep it in his aquarium like a pet. Maybe he'd grow to love it so much, giving it up would seem like the right thing to do.

He decided to give his census one last shot and paddled out to the edge of the pond. The mud gave way to an expanse of rippling sand. Sometimes serpents battled here at night, but now the scene was empty. Mons watched the setting sun turn the shadows from left to right.

The window at the bottom of his boat kept fogging up. The water was so cold and his breath was so hot. He kept wiping away the fog, but there was a dull red patch that wouldn't go away. It grew bigger and bigger until it could be seen to swarm.

Krill!

They zipped and unzipped along wavy lines. Soon, they were bumping against the glass and Mons could see the deadness of their eyes and the madness of their legs.

One million krill, he wrote with a shiver. If each gave only one pearl eye or coral leg, the treasure would be enormous. But the krill paid no attention to Mons. They churned the water, squealing like Styrofoam until Mons swooned.

The krill fell silent. Mons opened his eye. A blue shadow was carving a wedge through the swarm. The whale's head breached the surface, trailing sheets of baleen. Its striped cheeks ballooned as it took in tons of krill. It dove with a tail slap that almost turned over Mons' boat.

After three decisive strikes, the krill were gone. The whale's final charge sent it far up onto the beach. Only its tail remained in the water, bobbing listlessly.

Mons pulled his boat up next to the whale. He ran his finger along its side. It felt like canned beets.

"Does that tickle?" he asked. "I'm sorry."

"Ohhhhh," the whale groaned. "I'm far too sick to care."

Mons sat in the sand near the whale's rheumy eye and tried to avoid staring. It was easy for Mons to give the impression of staring.

"You didn't look sick just now gulping down all that krill," he said encouragingly.

"They were poisoned."

"Who poisoned them?" Mons asked.

"They poison themselves. It's their idea of revenge." The whale groaned again, making the sand jump like fleas. "I knew they were poisoned after the first bite but I couldn't stop myself. I was in a feeding frenzy."

"Is there no antidote?" Mons asked.

"None that I know of," the whale said.

"What should we do?"

"I'm going to wait here until I die."

"Me too," Mons said. "I mean," he blushed, "I think you're far too big to die."

He sat down at a polite distance from the whale's eye. A gull landed and Mons shooed it away. Without intending to, he began to hum.

"If you want to help," the whale said, "you could drip some water in my eyes. They're beginning to stick."

While Mons bathed the whale's eyes, it told him some of its best qualities. It could kill three sharks with a single blow. Its spout could bring down low-flying planes. It had three daughters: Baleine, Adelaide, and Arugula. Arugula had been eaten by killer whales, but her elder sisters were happily married and wintering as usual near Antarctica. The whale was especially fond of krill, even for a whale, and was known for its beautiful singing voice, which could be heard five hundred miles away.

"I'd love to hear you sing sometime," Mons said, "when you're feeling better. My mother also has a beautiful voice . . ."

"Please keep talking," the whale said.

Clearly, the whale wanted to be distracted so Mons forced himself to go on and on: "She sings when we have guests, or when she's sad and lonely. She plays every instrument except the flute, which contorts a person's face. We are very proud of her face. Once, she gave a recital for the Queen and was rewarded with a castle, Maurixiana, which doesn't actually exist. But it's still a great honor. However you should never pay her compliments because . . . Whale? Whale?" Mons stroked its forehead. The whale was dead.

Mons began to cry. His tears tasted like olives, tumbling down his dusty face. Soon, he was too thirsty to cry anymore. He ate some pink jelly, which restored his blood sugar and made him brave. He used a piece of driftwood to prop open the whale's mouth and climbed down its throat.

The esophagus was slimy but ridgy. As he crawled, the warm weights of organs pressed down on him. Fragments of krill squealed under his knees.

The stomach itself was just tall enough for Mons to stand up in. The krill gave off a magenta glow, by which Mons could make out three gold rings hanging from the ceiling. He laced his arms through one of them and swung until the flesh tore, dropping him into a mountain of krill. He did the same thing with the other two rings, then looped all three over his arm.

Ever since his adenoid surgery, Mons had not had a keen sense of smell, yet even he was beginning to feel queasy from the stench of shrimpy bile. He slithered back up the esophagus but was disappointed to find his way blocked by the tongue. Swelling with rigor mortis, it had snapped his driftwood brace.

"Help!" Mons shouted, but his voice was muffled by the sheets of baleen. He lay back in the soft, foul darkness and began to abandon hope. Then he noticed a speck of daylight above him. Two specks. They must be the whale's blowholes. Using his rings to dilate the larger one, Mons wormed his arms up until they stuck, and he began to be sucked upward by capillary action.

Unless you can remember being born, it will be difficult for you to imagine Mons' sensations during this process. At last, his head popped into the air, but his body remained stuck so tight he could hardly breathe.

Freja, wearing a dress with white flowers on it, was carving flesh from the whale's side with a knife.

"What are you doing?" Mons croaked.

"It looks as if you need my help," Freja said.

The more he needed it, the more it would cost him, so Mons said as casually as possible, "I feel quite cozy actually. Maybe I'll stay here all day."

"Maybe you'll stay there for the rest of your life." With a grunt, Freja pulled out a rib. "At last! I was beginning to think the beast was all fat."

"The beast had a name," Mons said reproachfully, although he couldn't remember what it was.

"Corpy, Tubbuluent, or perhaps Gross-Beast?" Freja said.

"That isn't kind, Freja. Whales have lovely names like Adelaide or Arugula."

But Freja could smell other people's secrets.

"I'll let you out," she said, "if you give me half of whatever it is you're hiding."

Mons knew it would be wrong to share the whale's rings with Freja. It would just be so wrong. But as the sun was getting hotter, the blowhole was getting tighter...

"Fine," he said, and Freja plunged her knife into the whale's head. Nothing happened.

"I was hoping to strike the sneezing cortex," she explained, "and make you fly out of there like a cannon ball."

"Perhaps that only works on live whales," Mons said. "Or if you had an electric knife oh dear!" Freja had begun to hack madly around the blowhole. Mons fell onto the sand in a slurry of fat and blood that smelled strangely of violets. The rings slipped into the surf, which washed them clean.

"Real gold!" Freja said. "You can almost smell it."

The gold was daffodil yellow and so soft that Mons' fingers left marks on it. Each ring had geometric designs like the imprints of seashells.

"Just think what I can buy!" Freja said. "A Mercedes, for instance, or a cat."

Mons was thinking what a fine present one of these rings would make for the Morra. As he admired the designs on the rings, however, he accidentally deciphered their code. The shell prints were a form of writing. The whale had left each of her children a poem. Unfortunately almost everything was lost in translation:

Baleine
Oooooo
I love you

Adelaide
you resemble
a tram

Arugula
watch out for
Killer Whales

"This is not our gold," Mons said sadly. "It is the inheritance of whales."

"What does a whale need a ring for?" Freja asked.

"If Arugula had had hers earlier, she might still be alive."

"Well, it's no good to her now," Freja said. She grabbed Arugula's ring. Before she could grab the others, Mons threw them into his boat, hopped in, and drifted out to the center of the pond. He dropped the rings overboard. Before they vanished they turned a rich, mysterious green.

"Don't think I won't dive for them," Freja said.

But she didn't.

Back home, she melted her ring in a saucepan and poured out the drops on a cookie sheet, stamping each with a coin bearing a portrait of the Queen. When it had cooled, Freja shook her stash into a pile under her bed.

"Now I will sleep like a dragon," she purred. "Just try sneaking into my room at night. I mean it."

Reluctantly, Mons promised that he would.

The guests at dinner were Lunka Lunka, Joe and Juan, and a small Samantha that Mom had taken on as a boarding student to learn music and the art of conversation. She watched the others with awestruck eyes.

Dad began by giving Mons some advice: "Every day you should try out a new profession."

"Try the easy ones first in case you like them," Lunka Lunka said.

"Today I administered a census," Mons said.

"We don't need any more of that—excuse me—surveillance," Joe said, exchanging a look with Juan.

"It was just of the pond," Mons said.

"Seriously, it frightens me the information they're collecting about us these days," Juan said.

"What did your census reveal?" Mom asked Mons.

"Well, there were seven Pricklers less than last year—or 'fewer,' do I mean? The turtle is doing good, or do I mean 'well'?" The Samantha's presence made Mons feel like he was failing an exam. "For a while there was a whale, but it died almost before it could tell me its life's story."

"Whales! Everybody's in love with whales these days," Joe said.

"Always, moaning, moaning, moaning," Juan said.

"I quite like whales . . ." the Samantha said.

"Can you repeat your sentence so that everyone can hear?" Mom said.

The Samantha looked flustered, and Mons was going to say something to cover for her, probably "Sorry," when the doorbell rang.

A policeman came in and said, "Sorry for interrupting but I've been looking for these characters for a long time." He put Joe and Juan into his car and drove away.

Mons felt relieved, but Mom said, "It's too bad Joe and Juan couldn't stay for Mons' jelly." She brought it out on a crystal plate. Seemingly as an afterthought, she tossed two giant sugarfly wings into the air and set them on fire as they drifted down and draped themselves over the plate.

"How beautiful," the Samantha said, pale with delight.

The jelly was both hot and sour, and it was fun to break the crust with your spoon.

"I almost forgot. Before we turn in," Mom said, "does anyone have any gold or jewels we can throw the Pricklers as funeral gifts? I'm sorry we didn't hear about their loss at the time."

"I have an earring, but it's too big," Dad said shyly.

"I don't own anything valuable," the Samantha said.

Solemnly, Lunka Lunka unfastened his collar. He took off the license and placed it in the center of the table. "It isn't much," he said, "but my dying grandma said it was real tin."

"Where's Freja?" Mom asked.

Freja had slunk away halfway through the meal. Perhaps only Mons, long used to keeping one eye open for her, had noticed. "Counting her coins, I bet," he said, then clapped his hands over his mouth. How easy it had been to betray her!

Mom marched up the stairs and returned with a pillowcase full of coins. Freja followed on her hands and knees, sobbing and tearing her hair.

"She has so much self-confidence," the Samantha said admiringly.

That night, Mons rowed out to deliver the Pricklers' gifts. The moon seemed to be made of paper, and his boat tore it into strips.

"I wouldn't have expected throwing away treasure to feel so good," he said, pouring the coins away. They disappeared with a greenish twinkle, but Lunka Lunka's license landed on a rock.

He parted with the sapphire last of all. Perhaps it was rude of him to return a gift. On the other hand, he assumed the Pricklers had given him the thing they would have been happiest to receive. It sank invisibly for a few seconds, then flared blue, continuing to glow until it disappeared from view, or else grew so small you couldn't tell it from the stars.

The Ruby Cloud

MONS WOKE FROM a dream in which he'd made friends with a middle-aged woman at the library to the sensation of someone sitting on his stomach. Perhaps a squirrel had crept in to stare at him while he slept. But when he sat up, nothing went skittering out the window. There, the moon hung like a phosphorescent mask and the Goodall sat in the branches of the Great White Birch, humming a familiar tune with made-up words. They were silly but also sad and went something like this:

> *The lizard on the fountain cried*
> *the night his lizard mother died.*
> *His snowy scales turned black.*

The owl that ate him, black inside,
ne'er flew home again, again
she ne'er flew home again.

The owlets in their snowy nest
sighed into their feathered breasts
*   and knew they were alone*
'til one by one they fell asleep
and forgot about their home, their home
forgot about their home.

My love he climbed the mountain white
to beard the lizard in its den
*   and ne'er come home again.*
Too proud to hear his lover's call
his heart has turned to stone, to stone
his heart has turned to stone.

Now I climb your tree at night
to test the ripeness of the moon.
*   Yes, I could pluck it if I liked*
and turn our gladness into bone.
Yet we would be alone, my love
still we would be alone.

The song ended with a howl that made Mons' hair stand on end.

"You'll wake up Dad!" he said. But Dahl's howl—still in progress—was somehow secret, made of wavelengths only Mons could hear.

Finally, Dahl dropped in and said, "What's wrong with your stomach?"

Mons ran his hands over the mysterious bulge, relieved yet disturbed to find it was only skin.

"Did you eat anything unusual for dinner?" Dahl asked.

"Just some pink jelly."

"I have something to show you," Dahl said, eyes shining. "Run!"

In his hurry, Mons fell down the tree. He landed on a pink cloud that vanished with a shattering sound.

"These clouds are everywhere," he said.

But Dahl was already gone. He was bigger, stronger, and smarter than Mons. But Mons didn't mind.

He chased Dahl to the pond, where a patch of water bubbled pink. The steam thickened into clouds which drifted toward the mountain.

Migrating, Mons thought.

Dahl took off his clothes. He was in such a hurry, he had trouble with his socks. He ran into the sea, stepping high to avoid the cold. When he reached the bubbles, he dove and stayed under a long time.

Showoff, Mons thought. But soon it occurred to him that Dahl had gotten stuck under a rock and was running out of breath. Mons hurried out, hardly noticing when his shoes were swallowed by the muck. His belly was as buoyant as a beach ball. Struggling to look down over it, he felt it slip up around his ribs and settle on his back, holding him face-down underwater.

On the seafloor, he saw a snake so long it had no head or tail. It was going into one hole and coming out another. Its skin was the same texture as the sand, and Mons would never have noticed it at all if it hadn't been moving so fast. But he didn't have long to look because Dahl was dragging him back to shore. The bubble was forced back up onto his belly. He felt indescribably gassy, but on the whole it was less embarrassing on this side.

Dahl was saying, "I chased this songbird through the water. It kept letting me get closer, turning around and chirping like we were playing a game. But every time I reached for it, it exploded in a flurry of bubbles and two new birds darted off in opposite directions. I chased them but the same thing happened every time. And wherever the bubbles touched my body, look—"

There were shiny blotches on Dahl's chest. His hands were coated with the same substance. When he twiddled his fingers, it cracked.

Mons took a piece. It tasted like jam.

"I'm going to catch one of those clouds in a jar," Dahl said.

"Oh!" Mons said. "Be careful not to breathe it."

Dahl ran into the forest. Mons lost sight of him but guessed he was taking the deer path to the foot of the mountain where they used to perform false sacrifices.

Panting, Mons found Dahl perched on the ceremonial stone, raising a branch over his head. A frightened-looking cloud was edging around the base of the rock.

But just as Dahl was about to strike, the sun peeked over the hill. The cloud turned white and vanished. It took a long time for it to fade from Mons' eye.

Dahl slumped.

"I didn't have a jar anyway," he said, breaking his stick.

"Well, maybe next time," Mons said. He climbed onto the rock. "Do you want to sacrifice something?" he asked.

Dahl smiled. "I have to go to Östersund," he said. "Aunt Siv is getting a new dog."

"How long will you be gone?" Mons asked casually.

"Until Friday."

It must be hard to sound unexcited about visiting Aunt Siv.

A gunshot in the woods made Mons' belly jiggle.

Dahl jumped up.

"Bye!" he said. After a few bounds, he turned around. "Stay indoors at night," he said. "I've seen a lot of tracks around."

"Oh," Mons said. "Where exactly?"

But Dahl was already gone.

Going home always took longer than going away, especially when the forest was so full of frolicking squirrels and things. Mons saw a moose guiding her daughter over the creek. Hiding from them, he found one of those red mushrooms with white dots. As he picked it, a familiar chill washed down his spine. The forest had become as quiet as the bottom of the sea.

He closed his eye and prayed for the Morra to come. But the minute passed, and the birds began to sing. Mons opened his eye. The mushroom he was holding had turned to glass.

Lunka Lunka was dozing in the hammock on the sunny side of the house, his notebook lying open on the grass. Mons picked a cluster of rowan berries and considered chucking them at Lunka Lunka's head. He wished Lunka Lunka were a puppy again.

"Will you kiss my nose?" he asked.

"Sure. You taste better than usual," Lunka Lunka said.

"Thanks," Mons said.

"I have a small poem for you," Lunka Lunka said.

> *Let every crawling thing*
> *with tail*
> *tune its lyre.*
> *Let snail*
> *blow its horn to spring.*

Well, what do you think?"

Mons hesitated. If it were somehow about Lunka Lunka's childhood, then you had to be careful. But he couldn't help laughing.

Lunka Lunka bit him.

"Sorry," Lunka Lunka said, "but it was about my childhood."

Everyone at breakfast had an opinion about Mons' stomach. Mom said he couldn't have syrup: "You're just at the age when a boy is beginning to get fat."

"I was never fat as a boy," Dad reminisced.

"My uncle believed fat people were kinder," Lunka Lunka said.

"What's inside, I wonder?" Freja prodded him with her knife.

"I mean my uncle who resembled the composer Janáček," Lunka Lunka said. "Not the one who *claimed* to be Maltese."

"Dahl went to his Aunt Siv's," Mons said. Did he expect the others to be sad?

"I wish he'd told me so I could have asked him to buy sweaters," Mom said.

"It never got this cold when I was young," Dad said.

The bubble shifted in Mons' stomach. He felt giddy at the thought of being eaten by the Morra. Perhaps that was why he was getting so fat—his body was preparing itself for her. He excused himself and ran outside to lie down on the grass.

Freja followed him. "The same thing happened to my mother," she said, "just before my brother was born. She got as fat as the moon, and you know what was inside of her? *My brother himself. There was a little man inside of her.*"

"How awful," Mons said.

"Yes," Freja said, trotting her fingers up Mons' stomach.

Mons napped with Lunka Lunka under his arm until Mom started playing "Servant Ruprecht," which meant he was wanted in her study right away.

As he waited for Mom to finish, he studied the portrait of the Queen hanging on the wall. She looked as if she were very pleased with something she had eaten.

Mom let the final chords die away, then said, "Would you like to go to Östersund all by yourself?"

It was too much. Of course he wanted to, but . . .

"Can't you or Dad come?"

"We have to work," Mom said. "You could stay at a hotel and buy some sweaters for the rest of us. Choose the patterns yourself. I thought it might be fun and educational for you."

There were so many things that might go wrong! The bus driver might not understand his language. The hotel might have gone out of business, forcing him to sleep in a clothes store inside some clothes. Worst of all, Dahl might look at him like, "Can't you see that Aunt Siv is *my* special thing?"

"I'm just so small . . ." Mons said.

"Alright," Mom said. "I should have known it was too much for you."
She turned back to her piano.

Mons stayed for a long time, listening to her play.

Afterward, he wandered along the highway in the direction that seemed
to have the most butterflies in it. The most roadkill, too. He wasn't even
sure where this highway led but it must have been somewhere OK because the cars were driving there very fast. As the clouds thickened, so
did Mons' guts. The first drops of rain seemed to be falling down a well.

He took shelter under a larch. It was full of holes and it soon became
apparent there was a boy on the other side. The larch belonged to him.

"But you can stay here till it stops raining," he said.

"Thank you," Mons said.

"Do you know why I'm hiding?" the boy said.

"No," Mons said.

"I was being chased by a monster," the boy said.

"How," Mons asked, "*big*?"

"Bigger than a bear," the boy said. "To be honest, I didn't get a good
look."

"No . . ." Mons said.

"Maybe it *was* just a bear," the boy said. "But the funny thing is—I
almost wish she'd caught me!"

Was he waiting for Mons to express surprise?

That night, Mons dreamed about a tyrannosaurus skull whose good
opinion once lost was lost forever. Around it swam translucent fish,
holding umbrellas in their ribs. They trailed black ripples through the
stars, and Mons woke up with the usual sensation of being watched.
The moon sat in his window.

"Dahl?" Mons said, mistaking it for his friend. Some pink gas twirled
out of his mouth. "Oh!" he said, and his stomach squealed like a balloon
as the whole cloud escaped. It spiraled to the ceiling and began to rain.

Mons caught the drops in the ice cream bowl he kept by his bed. The water twitched like syrup on the boil, shrinking and darkening. With a shattering sound, it crystallized, leaving a ruby the size of a plum. There was a flickering inside, like a moth tossing itself against window panes.

He held the stone, which was not only warm but seemed in need of comforting. He licked it. It tasted like jam. He slept with it in his arms, mostly to protect it from Freja but partly to fall more deeply in love with it so that it would seem like more of a sacrifice when the time came to give it up.

The Boy in White

MONS' NEW RUBY brought him courage, and the next morning he decided to tell Mom that he wanted to go to Östersund, after all. Then Madame Zingaressi arrived with her three sons. They were here on business. The youngest was only a couple years older than Mons. He wore white shorts, had white hair, and amused everyone with his friendly gossip and croaking laugh. The second son had red hair and a shiny red tie, and got along well with Dad, taking him by the arm into his study, where Mons believed they were making lots of money. The eldest son was all dressed in black, except for the silver buttons on his shirt. He said almost nothing, and Mons got the impression he was either the family's mastermind or its prisoner.

Madame Zingaressi herself had *extremely* wrinkly skin. The wrinkles did not follow any facial expression Mons knew of, but rather covered her whole face evenly like some expensive kind of cloth. She wore a strapless gown and slouched around like a teenager. Without saying anything impolite, she managed to make everyone feel like they were going to die. "An aura of impending doom," Dad had once said, was the secret to the Zingaressis' success. Given the end of the world, people would sell at any price.

Did it work on him?

During the three days of negotiations, Mons' job was to keep the boy in white from feeling sad. This was easy. The boy in white thought everything Mons said was clever. Soon, Mons was showing him things that only Dahl knew about, such as the mudslide, the swan's nest, and the game where you made boats out of flowers then waited for them sink.

On the second day, Mons and the boy in white were building cardhouses in the attic and telling funny stories about their classmates—well, only the boy in white was capable of telling funny stories, and Mons had never been to school—when the boy in white looked around like there might be a spy then took a jeweled bird out of his pocket. The bird had a black cap, white cheeks, and a red belly. Its wings were covered with diamonds. It was a family heirloom that opened, the boy said, "but Mom told me never to show anyone."

"OK," Mons said, averting his eye.

"But I'll show you anyway," the boy said. He popped open the bird's left wing and poured a golden snake into his palm. "It's a bracelet," he said, as if repeating an important lesson, "*not* a necklace. Hold out your hand."

The boy draped the snake around Mons' wrist. Mons couldn't tell how the head and tail went together, but they did and the bracelet became very tight.

"You can leave it on till tomorrow," the boy said with a smile.

"Thank you," Mons said, "but how do I take it off?"

The boy touched the snake cleverly in two places. It sprang apart with a hiss and curled up in his hand.

"Just let me know if you change your mind," he said.

The boy in white no longer seemed interested in cardhouses. He no longer seemed interested in Mons. Mons wished his mom had given him some magic heirlooms he could show the boy. "Wait here!" he said, and ran to his room.

But opening the door, he hit his head, and by the time he could think clearly again, showing his ruby to the boy in white no longer seemed like such a good idea. Instead, he chose the brontosaurus Dahl had carved for him out of wood. At first, it had been a stegosaurus but the spines hadn't turned out so well. It seemed like the most fascinating thing Mons owned, almost, but the boy in white was clearly disappointed. Still, he played with it for a while, making the appropriate sounds.

On their way downstairs, the boy in white slipped into the bathroom. Mons couldn't help noticing the boy in red was already there. And he couldn't help hearing the boy in red was speaking with a much less velvety voice than usual.

The next day, the boy in white avoided Mons. Mons felt like he spent all day being avoided. Under the circumstances, it was hard to get any reading done.

After dinner, Madame Zingaressi said she would tell everyone's fortunes.

"One at a time, please," she said, going into Dad's study.

Freja emerged from her consultation looking pleased. "Everything will go just as I planned," she said. "I wouldn't look so optimistic if I were you."

Returning from his interview, Lunka Lunka curled up sadly on the ground. "I don't want to talk about it," he said.

Mons hoped she hadn't told him he would never be a famous poet.

Mom went in just to be polite. She didn't believe in magic.

Dad tried to look inscrutable after his séance but was obviously pleased with himself.

Was it really wise to do business with a woman who could see the future?

Finally, it was Mons' turn. He didn't insist on going last; the others just let him. The study seemed smaller and smokier than usual. Madame Zingaressi sat in a green halo, and when Mons sneezed, she crossed herself.

"Disfigured child," she said, "what do you wish to know?"

Mons hadn't expected to have to ask questions.

"I don't know..." he said. "How's Dahl?"

"'Dahl' is fine," she said, putting his name in quotes. "Anything else?"

Mons decided to risk it.

"Is the Morra real?" he asked.

Madame Zingaressi didn't look surprised. But she wouldn't, would she?

"Yes," she said.

"Where can I find her?" Mons asked.

"In the forest."

"I *knew* it."

"But soon she will go into the mountain. And later—she will come to your house."

Mons swallowed.

"Is it true she's getting bigger?" he asked.

Madame Zingaressi pressed her fingertips together.

"Next time you see her, you won't even recognize her. Now, our time together has come to an end."

Mons thought that was a beautiful way to say goodbye. She coughed and opened her hand. He shook it, then realized she was asking for a tip. He wished his parents had raised him better. The only thing he had was Dahl's brontosaurus. He offered it to Madame Zingaressi, but she refused to touch it.

"Don't be silly," she said. "If you have no silver, then a curse be on your house." She looked quite friendly. Mons wished he knew whether she were kidding about the curse.

He went upstairs to return his dinosaur. Opening his bedroom door, he hit the boy in white.

"I was just coming out," the boy in white said, as if he didn't want to be suspected of eavesdropping.

Mons wanted to explain that he would never suspect anyone of anything, as long as they were nice to him, but the boy ran downstairs. Mom and Dad were helping the Zingaressis into their color-coded coats. The boy in white immediately said something that made everyone laugh.

"Mons," a shadowy voice said. It seemed to come from inside his head. The boy in black was standing behind him, so close Mons could see the bristles on his chin.

"Take these," he said, and Mons felt something warm in his hands, then something cold. The warm thing was his ruby. The cold thing was a silver ring in the shape of a heron. It was flying around the moon.

"Thanks," Mons said.

"Where's Bruno?" the red-lipped brother said. "Ah, there you are!" he said, taking the boy in black by the arm. "It has been a *very* successful trip."

The Cannibal Queen

FROM THEN ON, Mons wore the eldest brother's ring around his thumb, since all his other fingers were too small. He considered it a charm against disease, considering what happened next.

Sister Phyllis was Patient Zero. She'd forgotten her wimple, walking in the rain, and soon the nuns were sneezing each other off their feet. Drømö Church advised people to pray alone. Children began glowing with a fever that sometimes left only a pile of bones. Soon, every house wore a yellow sash, and a yellow ribbon dangled from every tree. The squirrels caught fire as they ran from bough to bough. The swallows disappeared mid-swoop in puffs of smoke. The opera didn't close until every singer had lost her voice. Brunhilde breathed so much fire it turned the ceiling brown.

The Rastroms blamed Russian germs. The Hundbirgs accused their cows. The Ylléns dusted off legends about a recurring season of coldness, famine, and disease. Mom trusted the official explanation—flu—and Mons pretended to agree. But in his heart he believed in the Gypsy's curse. And when his own family, last of all, succumbed, he felt betrayed. He had thought the Gypsies liked them better than the others. Still, his ring seemed to keep him personally safe.

Cooking for the invalids, Mons and Freja made lots of pancakes. Freja broke the eggs, giving each one a personality and matching crime as she marched it toward the bowl.

As Mons fed him, Dad kept saying strange things like "Let's make friend fries" or "I'm a self-saucing cake." Mons tried hard to comply with all his father's reasonable demands.

Yet Dad was lucid compared to Lunka Lunka, who could only shiver and whine like a blunted saw. It was sadder when dogs got sick.

While chopping a cucumber, Freja suggested bleeding Dad.

Reluctantly, Mons agreed.

Dad whimpered as they approached. Freja didn't bother to conceal her juicy blade.

"He's delirious," she said mournfully, and Mons held his father down while she rolled up his sleeve.

"It's for his own good, right?" Mons said, looking away.

At that moment, Mom played the chords which meant, "Drop everything and come to me." Freja dropped her knife, narrowly missing Mons' feet.

Mom was sitting at her piano, picking out a lonely melody amidst a mountain of Kleenex. "I just got a letter," she said, gesturing toward the open window. "They have the medicine we need in Östersund."

"Are you delirious?" Freja asked hopefully.

"Do you need me to go to Östersund?" Mons said. "You think I can do it alone?"

"Yes. Just give me a second to put on my swimsuit," Mom said. She leaned forward until her head rested on the edge of the piano. Then she began to snore.

. . .

Mons needed money to pay for the medicine. He looked in Mom's purse, Dad's desk, and the safe whose password was "I love children." But the money was gone. So he took his ruby instead. He hung it around his neck in a pouch. It wasn't heavy except when he tried to take it off.

Walking to town, he laid out his plan: "We'll take the bus if it's still running. Otherwise we'll borrow someone's bike."

"There's more sinners going to heaven," Freja said, pointing to the black column rising over the church.

A trail of ants caught fire at their feet, burning like a fuse all the way back to their hole in the ground. Mons felt a muffled boom.

Their Queen, he thought.

In the Ylléns' driveway, a lilac tricycle turned a circle in the wind.

"That belongs to other children," Mons scolded as Freja stole it, pedaling with her knees up to her ears.

"I don't like it, anyway," she said. "A disgusting color."

"Yes," Mons said wistfully. It had a silver bell and white ribbons sprouting from the handlebars. It was almost too beautiful to look at.

"You can take it if you want," Freja said mockingly.

"Oh, no," Mons said. But he wavered. He took it. After all, the Ylléns didn't need it anymore, and he had to travel as fast as possible. Mom's life might depend on it.

"Which way is Östersund?" Mons asked.

"The highway only goes in two directions. Pick one. Just drop me off at home first," Freja said, tripping over nothing and sitting on the ground. "Suddenly I don't feel good."

The road to Östersund got steeper and steeper. Soon, Mons was too tired to pedal, so he walked alongside his trike, ringing the bells to cheer himself up.

At the top of the fell, he looked out over the heather, rusty where it had ceased to bloom. Here and there, steam rose from hidden springs.

He coasted into the forest down the backside of the hill. Pine cones tore under his wheels, emitting a lovely smell. Tiny butterflies began to land on his arms and face, getting bigger and bluer until he could hardly see. He was reluctant to wipe them off, though. He didn't want them to stop liking him. But he suspected they liked him less for himself than for the ruby glowing under his shirt.

He drove into a tree and the butterflies vanished in a shower of dust. His front wheel was bent out of shape, and something inside him beeped anxiously as if to say, "Don't look up!" where a squirrel sat on a hand-lettered sign labelled "Medicine." The squirrel was wearing a chef's hat with the royal crest on it.

"Are you the doctor?" Mons asked.

The squirrel screamed.

"Everyone at home is sick," Mons explained.

The squirrel dropped onto Mons' handlebars, and Mons ran away.

He tripped over roots and stones. Larvae slithered down his face as he extracted it from puddles. Red ants trickled after him, swelling up around his shoes whenever he paused for breath. Why did they make him crush them? They flecked his legs like mashed potato.

He tumbled down a grassy hill, landing in front of a cave. "Dahl?" he shouted. The cave groaned and belched a billow of white flies. He screened his face with his hands and went in.

The first room contained a teal van with the royal crest on it. The windows were broken, the hood was smashed, and the stuffing had been torn out of the seats. There was no one inside.

As Mons went deeper, the daylight disappeared. He stepped into nothing and fell for a second, landing squarely on his back. He lay still, collecting his breath. The rock was strangely soft. He hoped his eye would adjust to the darkness.

"Dahl?" he called. There was no response. He sneezed, and jeweled lights in every color blinked on around him. Only after gazing at them for a long time did he realize they were embedded in large, clear spiders, picking their way slowly across the rock.

"You're lovely," Mons said with a shudder. He reached up to touch the one just above him. It hissed and fell, curling into a fist. All the others turned blue and flattened themselves against the wall. They dimmed and glowed in a wave that travelled down the tunnel.

Mons followed their light down many complex branchings of the cave until he arrived at a chamber full of firelight and smoke that did not smell as if it came from wood. He got quite close before he noticed the woman with veins on her face. She was sitting on a pile of bones, using what looked like a femur to stir the contents of a pot. It was large enough for a child to bathe in, and smoke fell over its rim in folds. The coals made ugly faces at him. And the smell! Mons had never imagined anything could be so disgusting and delicious at the same time.

"Who are you?" the woman said without looking up. Her hair sagged under a network of pearls. A crown glittered in her lap.

"Mons, Your Majesty."

"Have you come for Lunch with the Subjects?" she asked.

"Yes, please!" Mons said. "Where are the other Subjects?"

"It's not polite to ask royalty questions."

"No!" Mons laughed. "Sorry."

"How did you get here?"

"I rode my trike. It was quite a trip."

"Your forehead is bleeding," the Queen said, still without looking.

"That must have been when I fell," Mons said. "I saw your bus, by the way. I hope you weren't hurt?"

"That's almost a question. One more and you have to get in the pot."

"Oops!" Mons said.

"The monkeys brought me here," the Queen said. By *monkeys*, she presumably meant *squirrels*. "But then they had to go." She tasted her broth. "You don't sound well."

"I'm fine"—Mons coughed—"but my mother is sick. That's actually why I've come—"

"Your mother?" The Queen looked directly at him for the first time. "Yes, I see the family resemblance." She took a notebook out of her purse and scribbled something in it. "Have you ever been to camp?" she asked.

"No."

"My favorite part was cooking potatoes in aluminum foil. You'd bury them in the coals and when they were done, nothing was tenderer . . ."

Mons' grip tightened around the ruby in his shirt.

"Messy work, though," the Queen said. "You never knew if you were going to find them underdone, or charcoalized."

Mons swallowed.

"Are you the Morra?" he asked.

"So that's your last question?" She handed him her crown. "The answer is yes. And since you've been so brave, you can hold this while you cook. Hop in!"

He started to climb into the cauldron.

"Take your clothes off first," she said.

"Sorry!"

He felt the Morra watching as he folded his clothes neatly in a pile. Modestly, he kept his ruby out of sight, wrapping it in his shirt. The only thing he kept on was the Gypsy's ring, which had grown very cold.

There was a howl in the darkness. It was getting closer. It made Mons even colder. He had no time to spare.

He put one foot in the cauldron. The broth was boiling, yet it took him a second to feel pain. With a gasp, he fell in, hitting his forehead on the rim.

All around him were bones and teeth, meat and fur, shrouded in glistering fat. His ring flared white and melted, snaking over the broth in the shape of a bird. Suddenly, everything hurt less.

A handful of tablets landed on the fat. The Morra hefted her bone. "I take some pills with every meal," she explained. "It helps my heartburn."

She clobbered Mons' head, then began to poke at his collarbone. Mons realized he'd be too big to submerge unless you broke him up.

The howl sounded again, much closer, and Mons shared the Morra's irritation and dismay. Her look was enough to shatter a spoon. A pair of arms gripped him under the shoulders. The last thing he saw was a piece of tendon slipping out from between his toes.

. . .

He returned to his headache on top of the hill, where the moon had turned the grass to bone. He groaned, touching his head, then lay back in Dahl's lap. His vision was cloudy. Perhaps he'd never be able to see clearly again. He began to cry.

"She didn't eat me after all," he said.

"There, there," Dahl said.

Mons suddenly sat up.

"My clothes?" he asked.

"Right here."

He felt for the ruby. It was still in its pouch. He didn't mention it to Dahl.

"I got her purse," Dahl said modestly. He poured its contents on the ground.

There were fruit chews, a bottle of hand sanitizer labelled "Warning: I'm allergic," and a notebook of tiny drawings, apparently a catalogue of all the creatures she had eaten. It was mostly squirrels, but at the end was a drawing of Mons. It looked just like him.

Finally, there was the medicine.

"Open wide," Dahl said.

As Mons chewed, his tongue went numb.

"What's this?" he slurred, turning the last page in the Queen's notebook. It looked like a poem, but it was in Dahl's handwriting.

"Just something to keep me entertained while you were asleep . . ." Dahl said.

"Read it," Mons said. "Please."

In the distance, Mom could be heard playing "Wedding Day at Troldhaugen."

"Well . . . alright," Dahl said.

Mons' fever was cooling, but his skull still felt too small. He lay back, letting the moon soothe his eye, while Dahl read.

My love lies under a chestnut tree
  beside the quiet river
Where lisping winds like filigree
  make the blossoms shiver.

There, where the river bends to woo
  the reeds into a curl
My love sleeps gently on the grass
  as lonely as a girl.

And when the sky turns out its cup
  of evening on the sand
My love wakes with a sticky yawn,
  his sleep still on his hand.

"Mons?" Dahl asked. "Are you ready to go home?"
But Mons was fast asleep.

The Beauty Contest

THE NEXT MORNING was unexpectedly warm, so Mons and Freja went to stay at Denise's cabin by the Lake. Denise was the Samantha's older sister. She had a large cabin and wore hats to protect her beauty from the sun.

Mons and Freja were walking down the beach when Mons sank up to his knee in a seam of icy shells. On closer inspection, they turned out to be tiny crabs with feathery legs that thrummed like mad.

"They make my skin go ginky," Freja said.

A purple vein was spreading through the sand, faint from above but brilliant red wherever you scraped away the surface. Mons followed it to a stand of plum trees in the corner of Denise's garden. Their leaves were also turning red. Some were falling off.

"What's this?" Freja said, turning over a leaf. A Sooty was sitting cross-legged underneath.

"Can't you see I'm hiding?" it said.

"Look how dirty it is!" Freja said, picking it up by one leg. "It even makes the air dirty." She swung it around, leaving smudges.

"Are you hungry?" Mons asked the Sooty.

"Yes," it said. "But there's nothing good in anyone's cupboards." It bared its teeth: "But perhaps you don't like looking in other people's cupboards?"

"No, I love it," Mons said. "At least, I intend to do more of it in the future." Mom had ordered him not to let the Sooty feel vile. "But doesn't Denise buy groceries for you?"

"I don't live here anymore," the Sooty said. "I'm emigrating."

"Whatever for?" Mons asked.

"A mysterious woman has moved in next door and I'm not waiting around for What Happens Next."

"Who is this mysterious woman?" Mons asked. "And what happens next?"

"The sad part is I can tell you're not even being sarcastic," the Sooty said. For a moment it looked like it was about to confide. It glanced back and forth from Mons to Freja suspiciously, then dove back under its leaf. Its singing could be faintly heard:

> *Go away, go away*
> *Today's the day I go away*
> *And you will never smell me more*

Freja threw an armful of leaves at Mons. A slug slid down his face. Freja scooped up more leaves.

"Don't," Mons said. "It might not be safe."

"Not safe? Not safe?" Freja teased, bombarding him until he covered his head with his hands and ran away. He barely heard the last of the Sooty's song:

Today I go but you must stay
And I will never smell you more
Go away, O far away O

That night, while the Sooty was emigrating, Freja, Denise, Mons, and the Samantha lay on the roof, watching the stars.

"They're so pretty," Denise said.

"I don't know what a single one of them is called," Mons said. He hoped it didn't sound like bragging.

"I hate the idea of stars having names," Freja said. "It makes them less strange."

"You know what?" Denise said. "We should have a beauty contest and name the brightest star after the most beautiful person!"

The Samantha said "damn" in a voice so low, she seemed to think the others couldn't hear.

"I'll be the judge," Freja said.

"That's nice of you . . ." Denise said hesitantly. "But you have to play! The judge should be someone who could never win."

"You mean me?" the Samantha said.

"No, no," Denise said. "I mean Mons! Sorry Mons, but it's true, isn't it?"

"Yes," Mons said, and the contest began.

He looked at all the girls in turn. The Samantha was so self-conscious, it was painful to see. When he looked at Freja, she made the most disgusting face he had ever seen.

"Denise, you win," he said. "You are the most beautiful person."

"Gosh!" Denise said. "I never would have proposed the contest if I'd thought it would turn out this way."

"I'm not disappointed," the Samantha murmured, "because I never expected to win."

"So, from now on that big star is going to be known as 'Denise,'" Denise said, pointing into the sky.

. . .

The day after the beauty contest, it got so cold the spiders moved indoors. Mom invited Danglars, a recluse who carried a violin on his back, to sleep in the spare bed.

Given the chance, Danglars was fussy about his food. Mons made him spherical pancakes filled with jam. After sucking them dry, Danglars would leave them in a pile under his bed. Mons would collect them and refill them, but eventually they had to be thrown away.

One day, Danglars was sitting on the windowsill, knitting, when Mons asked him, "How long are you going to live here, Danglars?"

"Just till it gets warm again."

"I think that could be a long time," Mons said. He sat on the windowsill, taking care not squash Danglars.

"I wouldn't want to be outside on a day like this," Danglars said, pointing out the window. "See those footprints on the sand? Wherever that woman in yellow goes, things die."

"Oh, you mean Denise's new tenant?" Mons said. "She's kind of lovely, though." He was careful not to let anyone know how deep his fascination with the mysterious woman actually went. "Mom suggested I invite her to dinner, but I haven't had the courage to talk to her in person yet. Lunka Lunka thinks she goes under a nom de plume. Once, she poked her head into my treehouse—that is, the Goodall's and my treehouse—when we were drawing a map. She said 'whoosh' and the map turned yellow and cracked down the middle. All the leaves fell off and Dahl went south. Not emigrating—just to visit his aunt, you know, who got a new dog. Though I guess it's not so new by now . . ."

Danglars placed a comforting hand on Mons' leg. "I was often lonely as a child," he said.

Mons went into the garden to annoy the dog. His name was Lunka Lunka but he preferred to be addressed as "my learned friend." One of Mons' chores was to pick up his poop.

"Hello, Lunka Lunka," Mons said. "*The trees like old daisies are dropping their gold.* That's tetrameter in triplets. Won't you use it in your doggerel?"

Lunka Lunka snorted. "Everyone's a poet in this weather. It's that mysterious woman's fault."

"*The stranger cavorted*—No . . . *The stranger converted* . . ." Mons continued, counting the beats on his fingers.

The Samantha peeked out from under a leaf.

"Oh, hi, Samantha," Mons said. "You don't have to hide when it's just me."

"I know," the Samantha said, "but I do." She handed Lunka Lunka a piece of paper. "I've finished the assignment, Lunka Lunka. Please be kind."

"Your mother believes poetry will help the Samantha learn to speak her mind," Lunka Lunka told Mons. "But does she have a mind to begin with? My theory is she's been speaking it all along, only no one has noticed. Samantha, my sweet, have you remembered, above all, not to use the words 'flowers,' 'stars,' or 'madrigal'?"

"Perhaps," the Samantha said, a little defiantly.

"Read it to me," he said, and lay back to listen.

The Samantha read:

> *Come hour of cricket madrigal*
> *Greet the Season of the Leaf*
> *For you must fill my head with flowers*
> *Before we go to sleep.*

> *Come days of birdless afternoons*
> *And nights of cloudless stars*
> *We shall not live to see the moon*
> *Cross our cradle bars.*

> *O hand that turns the wave to ice*
> *And coats the leaf with rust*
> *Never take my heart from me*
> *Unless of course you must.*

Then let my heart unlearn its beat
My tongue let fall its key
My beauty drop around my feet
And drain into the sea.

"Go on," Lunka Lunka said.

"That's the end," the Samantha said. "Couldn't you tell?"

"I hope I don't need to point out those are exactly the same stanzas you wrote yesterday," Lunka Lunka said.

The Samantha looked at her feet. "I promise I tore up yesterday's poem and started over . . . But somehow there only seemed to be one thing to say."

"I'm sure you know how that feels, Lunka," Mons said.

"No," Lunka Lunka said. "I do not. Our ancestors have bequeathed us so many nice words besides 'heart' and 'flowers.' I wish you would try using some of them. Burn that nonsense, Samantha, and ask Mom for a clean sheet of paper. Tomorrow, I expect a poem of twelve pages on the joy of being a Greenland shark."

"I'll do my best," the Samantha said grimly.

Toward evening, Mons was wandering along the shore when he saw Freja and the Samantha making sand flowers. Freja pinched one together out of wet sand and laid it over one of the beach's veins. The petals flushed and curled.

With a cry of joy, Mons ran toward them, then noticed the mysterious woman at his side. Without knowing why, he smiled.

"It's good to see you," he said.

"Come with me," the Morra said, holding out her hand. It was soft and dry. "We need to talk about your ruby."

The Samantha was ready to plant her first flower. She placed it on the edge of a small vein so the color crept in only gradually, like a drop of blood in milk. The Samantha was delighted, but also—"I wish . . ." she said.

"Out with it," Freja said.

"I wish I were as pretty as you."

"What a dumb wish!"

That was exactly what the Samantha had been hoping she'd say.

Freja blew on her sand flower, frosting its petals with salt.

"Really," the Samantha whispered, "I think *you're* the one who should have a star named after her."

Denise was approaching with long steps.

"Are you two talking about boys?" she said. "I could tell from fifty yards away you were talking about boys." Her sundress streamed around her in the wind. She was so beautiful, the Samantha felt more love than hate. "Sand flowers!" Denise said. "Teach me to make the darling things."

"What can those two be talking about?" Freja said.

Mons and the mysterious woman were standing at the edge of the surf. The Samantha had never seen Mons look so glad.

"Don't get too close," she said as Freja headed off.

"I don't see why everyone thinks that mysterious woman is so wonderful," Denise said. She picked her sister's sand flower and held it under her nose. "She has a face like a dead leaf. Just look at her. What can Mons find to laugh about with someone so ugly?"

I've got it! the Samantha thought. She began to write a poem in her head.

> Come hour of cricket madrigal
> Greet the Season of the Leaf . . .

I know it's the same so far, she thought. But it may have a different ending.

Mons was finding it hard to give up his ruby.

"At first I only wanted it for your sake," he explained. "But then you were so odd. Now I don't see why I shouldn't keep it . . . It makes me warm." He cupped it in his hands, the light playing over his face like reflections from a pool.

"You really should give it to me," the Morra said, holding out her hand. "Otherwise terrible consequences will ensue!"

"I appreciate your argument," Mons said. "Let's just stand here and think about it for a while."

They huddled around the stone, growing warmer and warmer as the wind around them began to wail.

Freja approached, and Mons slipped the ruby back into its pouch. The Morra, who had grown to resemble a leafless tree, shrank back to human form.

"I heard you can read the future," Freja said. "Will you tell me how I'm going to die?"

"Sure," the Morra said.

Irritatingly, Denise was the only person who could pick sand flowers so they didn't die. The Samantha asked her to pick the prettiest one to give the mysterious woman as a present. Actually, she thought of it more as a peace offering. Hadn't they all misjudged her?

As the Samantha carried her treasure toward its goal, the mysterious woman bent down and whispered something into Freja's ear. Freja's hair turned white in a shimmering wave. Her clothes mottled and sprang apart at the seams.

The Samantha's flower turned back into sand and slipped through her fingers.

"I told you!" Denise said. "She's got the uglies, and they're catching!"

As the mysterious woman came toward them, Denise shouted, "Go away! I evict you from my beach house! I evict you from this beach! Oh, to think I could have rented my beach house to anyone so evil!"

But the mysterious woman didn't even look at her, and Denise lost her voice as she walked by.

Mons offered to help Freja up. She ignored him.

"Look at my hands," she said, showing off her knotty bones and clotted veins.

He looked. He couldn't think of anything to say.

"How old do you think I am?" Freja asked. "Seventy, eighty, *ninety?*"

"You don't seem very upset," Mons said.

"I don't think the age has had time to reach my brain yet." She waded into the surf to examine herself in the brief mirror of flooded sand. "There are benefits to being an old woman," she said. "For instance, I won't get in trouble for trespassing anymore."

Mons stood by her for a while.

"What did she tell you?" he said.

Freja looked at him with a smile.

"Do you really want to know?" she said.

"I guess not," Mons said, stepping back.

The Samantha was walking toward them, crying.

"I wish it had been me," she said.

The Housewarming Party

IT GOT COLDER than anyone could remember. Dahl called to say he was going to stay at his aunt's for another week—not because he had to, but because he enjoyed it so much there. Freja was in the hospital. Home was so lonely, Mons allowed the Samantha to teach him to play marbles.

Clink clink went the glass. The snow falling against the windows made no noise. Surely there ought to be a shattering sound? Mons didn't say anything encouraging for a long time, and the Samantha said, "I knew you wouldn't like this game."

"It's OK," Mons said. "So what do you want to be in five years?"

"Prettier and more popular," the Samantha said.

"Isn't that kind of shallow? I'm sorry," Mons said, but the Samantha had already disappeared.

He couldn't find her anywhere. He even went outside and looked among the pines, shivering, until he couldn't bear their silence anymore.

The next morning, Mom and Dad started putting their possessions into cardboard boxes. They started with the little ones. There were so many, Mom finally said, "Let's just burn them all instead."

Mons rescued his wooden flute then asked what was going on.

"We're moving," Mom said.

Dad was too ashamed to explain, so Mom said the deal with Madame Zingaressi had gone wrong. For instance, Dad had invested in summer wheat, among other things which seemed likely never to grow again.

Men arrived to count their things. Mom squabbled with them about the value of sheet music and canned fruit. She thought they were more valuable than the men did. Mons suspected his ruby might save the day, but still he kept it secret, hanging over his heart.

Danglars fled the house when the men came, apparently mistaking them for police. Mons never found out why Danglars was so afraid of police. Danglars was found frozen in the middle of the woods the next day. Mons found him.

"We'd have let him stay forever" was what the family carved on his tombstone. The ground was so hard they had to borrow the Transtömers' backhoe to dig the grave. Lunka Lunka composed an elegy, but it would be disrespectful to repeat it here. If you'd heard it, you'd understand why.

The men did not offer enough money to cover Dad's debt, so Mom arranged a silent auction. A sheet of paper was attached to every remaining object, as well as a pencil hanging by a string. Mons was sent around town to pay as many bills as possible and invite people to Mom's farewell party/auction.

The guests on arriving, however, seemed to regard it more as a declaration of surrender/yard sale. The Ylléns wanted to buy so many things, Dad had to sit at the green folding table all night, making change.

"Certain poets will have to find somewhere else to sleep all day," one

Tranströmer said to another, carrying a stack of china past Lunka Lunka, who sat on the steps wearing a red bow tie and greeting everyone who came in or out of the house because that was how he'd been raised.

The whole house had been opened for the party. Mom wanted everyone to see how it was before the new owners came. They were rumored to be an institution for children of some kind—punitive and edifying at the same time.

"Can you believe one family needed all this?" the mayor said to her husband as they toured the library. "Our children certainly turned out fine without so many books. Where are they anyway?" They were trailing along behind their parents like usual, but sometimes it was hard to tell the difference between them and empty space.

The Hundbirg kids at least were having a good time, drinking everything they could and guarding the cake. Their pet squirrels raced up and down the vines in the woodwork, breaking into convulsive laughter whenever they caught sight of themselves in the mirrors.

Mom had prepared a farewell recital but found the piano occupied by a group of Sister Phyllis' friends who wanted to buy it for their nunnery. "We want to hear the oldies," the oldest nun explained. "It's too bad none of us can play."

So instead of Schubert, Mom played "Tulip Time" and "Cloudy Wednesday," and the Sisters warbled along, endearingly out of tune. Mom seemed happy they were happy, but after everyone left she cried:

"I'm never going to play this piano again! That's just a statement of fact, not wounded pride."

So the debt was paid and the family had enough money left over to book two rooms for a week at the Thrice 9 motel on the outskirts of town. All the buses and taxis were out of service due to snow, so the family walked.

They packed before going to bed, and Denise's star was still shining when they began their trek along the highway, or at least where they remembered the highway had been.

It had been difficult deciding what to bring. With so little space, each object ought to be both practical and beloved. Mons took his chrysalis collection, thinking that if worst came to worst he could eat it. Otherwise, he could send the butterflies to carry the good news to all his friends. He was always planning to make a lot of friends in the near future.

Lunka Lunka brought only books, which he kept asking the others to carry. As the snow grew deeper, he had to throw them away, one by one. He kept only a notebook in which to record his sufferings. How he whined!

"Didn't you pack any dog food?" Mom asked.

"I didn't feel hungry at the time," Lunka Lunka said.

The worst part of the journey was the forest, which seemed to be full of animals caught in nets. They were actually fruits, and Mom cut one into wedges, but not even Lunka Lunka would try a slice.

Finally, they reached the motel. The owner didn't know them personally so their welcome was cold. So were their rooms, since nowhere in Drømö had ever had central heat. They draped every fabric they owned over Mom's plywood bed and all climbed in. The night was full of animal thumps and the smell Lunka Lunka gave off when he was scared.

The next morning, the motel management was gone. So were the other guests. The snow was so high you couldn't open the doors. You couldn't see out the windows except for an inch on top. Then that snowed over, too.

Occasionally, Mons climbed up the chimney and stuck his head out. But there wasn't much to see. The new animals were shyer than the old ones, even though they probably had less to be shy about.

The buffet area was full of powdered donuts, oatmeal packets, and things which added to the excitement of being trapped. On the whole, breakfast was a festive affair.

"At least we don't have to worry about getting kicked out at the end of the week," Mom said.

They made forts out of mattresses, raced down the halls, and used electric dryers to volumize their hair. Lunka Lunka became very good at accumulating a charge. They didn't even discover the basement until evening. Mons had never imagined there could be so many powdered donuts in one room!

Besides being able to go anywhere and do anything, it was nice not having to go anywhere or do anything, since everyone you loved was trapped in the same motel as you. Only Dahl was missing. Mons began to think he would never see him again, when Dahl fell down the chimney. A large package landed on his head.

"Thanks, Aunt Siv!" Dahl shouted up the chimney. Mons heard bells retreating. "She's going to deliver things to other people," Dahl said, "using her dog sled."

The package contained about six thick sweaters with gorgeous patterns like reindeer flying over the moon, firelit cottages at night, poppies, and some geometric patterns that Mons only now realized were meant to represent snow.

"Thank you," Mom said, giving Dahl a hug. Mons knew how much she loved sweaters.

"Did you get a cat?" Mons asked, frowning.

But it was only the Samantha, looking unsure of her welcome.

"My favorite student!" Mom said. "Where have you been?"

Dahl gave her a few seconds to answer, then said, "I found her under the sink. I went to your house because I didn't know you weren't there. I had to break an upstairs window to get in. I hope you don't mind."

"Well, it isn't our house anymore," Mom said.

"I thought I'd make sure you weren't all dead or something. But the whole house was empty except for a box of oats under the sink. Also a bar of soap, which smelled quite nice, and the Samantha. And some raisins. She was hugging the pipes even though they weren't warm anymore. It looked quite sad. She sang a song about her feelings. Can you remember how it goes?"

"No," the Samantha whispered. But Dahl's harangue seemed to have succeeded in giving her courage. "I always keep some raisins under the sink in case I have to hide," she said.

"That's very sensible," Dad said.

"But after the pipes went cold, it felt like the house had died. For a long time I thought *I* had died, and this was what happened next. Even when the Goodall showed up."

"Maybe we're all dead," Mons said.

Dad began to hand out sweaters, and soon everyone felt warmer. Dahl even knew how to light a fire using pieces of the front desk. It was the kind of thing your Aunt Siv taught you.

That night, Dahl tunneled from the lobby to the surface, and the next morning, the family found a full breakfast including roast squirrels and orange juice laid out for them in the buffet area. Dahl was cheerfully feeding the fire. He'd found the squirrels and oranges in the snow.

Mons' family spent the day decorating their rooms with identical motel things and mementos they'd brought from home. Lunka Lunka tried knocking out a wall to enlarge his room but that didn't work out very well. Everyone continued sleeping in Mom's bed at night.

Dahl made a sort of piano by filling bottles with varying amounts of water and stringing metal bars over them. The black keys were missing but Mom played "Good King Wenceslas" and other carols which now made more sense than ever before.

By the time the snow had stopped, Mons' family felt so at home in their new motel, they decided to walk to town with serving trays taped to their feet and invite all their friends to a housewarming party.

The town looked much better draped in ice, and all the horses had been set free. For once, it was actually fun talking with Mom's friends about the weather. When the kids had had enough, they went outside and bartered motel hot chocolate packets for grapes and other things that improved with cold. By 3 p.m., it was already dark and they had only two places left to go.

Mom's house—at first Mons thought it had been destroyed entirely, but this was just an illusion created by the general sense of danger and despair. In fact, it was much bigger than usual, with a sign out front reading "Mount Drømö Junior High." Mom looked at it for a long time but didn't go in.

Next, they went to the hospital, where Freja was in a sad state, trembling, bedridden, unable to speak. Although she didn't recognize them, she clearly wanted something, and Mons was infuriated that he couldn't figure out what it was. He took her hand and told her about the motel. "I wish you could come home with us," he concluded, but Freja had already fallen asleep, mouth and eyes both slightly ajar.

The nurse said Freja had been doing better until yesterday when she'd tried to escape and they'd had to put her on a different medication. Mom asked sternly for a sample but the nurse refused to give her one.

The next day, toward sundown, Mons and Dahl planted candles in the snow around their tunnel in order to help the guests find their way. The candles were labelled "Melody" and smelled OK.

At 5 p.m., the family gathered in the buffet area. They waited for a couple hours, sending Mons up every so often to check for figures on the horizon. But by eight o'clock, it was clear no one was coming. Mons assumed his family just wasn't popular enough, but Mom said, "If people are missing my party, something awful must have happened." She told everyone to collect things suitable for people in distress, and they set off for town.

The glow spread for miles over the snow. Despite the disguised landscape, Mons could tell it was coming from his home. He reached the top of the hill just after Mom, and saw the fire first reflected in her eyes.

It was quite beautiful. The snow slumped off the roof into a moat of meltwater. The rain gutters melted and ran away in snakes. A golden fish-scale pattern flashed rhythmically up through the shingles. Now and then, a window shattered, emitting a blurb of smoke that blackened as it left the light. The gawping neighbors made a ring of silhouettes around the flames. Were they dancing? With a crack, the central beam fell in, pulling the rest of the house around it like a tent.

Mons hugged his mother's waist. It would have been hard to say how long they stood there, watching, but when the flames were gone and the rubble still glowed, Mom said, "Let's go home."

The earth steamed around the house. Cinders gleamed in the soil. For the moment, winter was gone, and the neighbors were eager to help. The Rastroms offered to lend Mom their horses. The Hundbirg children had the idea of digging a pit, but didn't make much progress with just their hands. The Ylléns brought a fruitcake that no one felt like eating.

Mons poked through the rubble with a stick, trying to find anything of value. The ruby on his chest grew hot.

Dad and Mrs. Tranströmer speculated that the Zingaressis had burned the house down for insurance. Everyone agreed the remains belonged to Mom.

"We'll have to rebuild," she said, putting a hand on Mons' shoulder. "Why don't you and Dahl draw up some plans?"

"You'd really let us?"

"After all, you're going to be living here longer than anyone, I hope."

"Can we make everything just like it was?"

"You can try," Mom said. "But I thought maybe something smaller, closer to the Lake. Imagine how it will look covered in snow . . . You must have some ideas of your own," she added with a smile.

A fireplace, a turret, a rocking sofa bed. Stained glass, an aviary, and lots of places to hide. Above all, a slide from top to bottom of the house. Mons needed Dahl's help, but Dahl was nowhere to be found.

Had he gone into the forest? This was hardly the time for getting lost. Mons walked around the pond, shouting Dahl's name. He wondered if the water had frozen from top to bottom, or bottom to top.

Was he really never going to see Dahl again?

There was a person lying between the birches where Mons liked to fish. She'd made a crater in the snow. Mons rolled her over, careful to support her head. It was bald and black. Her face was one purple burn. She didn't seem to be alive. He tried to brush the ashes off her brow, but they were stuck as fast as bone.

Mons' ruby burned him through its pouch. He dangled it at arm's length, shading his eye. He dumped it on the snow. It bounced—or rather hopped—onto Freja's chest. Her eyelids fluttered. There was a flash, a crack. Something swallowed the moon. Wind blew from the forest, and Mons knew the Morra was near.

"Please," he said.

After a long white moment, Mons opened his eye. The wind was empty and his vision was clear. Freja sat up and the ruby, just a pebble, skittered off her chest. She lifted her hands and peeled off her mask. Her skin was smooth. Healthy red drops welled up here and there. Her eyes turned toward Mons in confusion but no pain.

She tore off the rest of her shell one piece at a time. She'd always liked that kind of thing. She was so beautiful Mons had to look away. Large snowflakes began to fall. As they landed on Freja's arms, she gasped with relief.

"Do you think they'll cancel school tomorrow?" she asked.

"Yes," Mons said, and it didn't feel like a lie.

The Little Mermaid and Me

AND ALSO MY cousin Eskild, who drowned off the west coast of Storsjön in 2013. I like to think it was a gentle way to go. Early that morning, his friends still asleep in the cabin where they'd gathered to build a midwinter bonfire, he walked toward the edge of the ice until it broke. Perhaps he swam, but not toward shore. He probably went numb before going unconscious. His body probably went to sleep before it began to drown. I like to imagine it romantically: Eskild looking straight up through the ice. His fingers rise toward mine. His hair wreaths his face as he sinks away—it's very cinematic. Poulenc's *Française* plays in the background. The body is refrigerated until they dredge it up, so there's no bloating. At the viewing, he looks more beautiful than ever.

Well, *actually*, instead of drowning off the west coast of Storsjön in

2013, what happened was Eskild got married in the Stockholm temple, then had a reception at Grandma Astrid's house. There was a cake covered with gummy bears, a second cousin playing Taylor Swift arranged for harp . . .

Let's just pretend he drowned.

In my earliest memories of Eskild, there's little to see: just the rafters overhead, birch shadows on the wall. Our beds smell like the fireworks Grandma keeps beneath them, and the stress of this weekend or summer day is over: I no longer have to entertain him; I just have to listen.

On stormy nights, when the trees are clawing the roof, he grows especially talkative, trying to overcome his fear of thunder, it seems, by listing everything he knows or believes to be true.

Finland has more islands than Canada. An elephant's skin is six inches thick. The second-most common cause of death for women in colonial America was burning alive. Because they were witches? *No*—because their skirts caught fire.

We subscribed to a magazine for children—*Muse*—that included one "False Fact" among its many truths. Usually, this was the most memorable information of all, the Fact part lingering long after its Falseness had faded.

According to *Muse*—perhaps—forgetting is essential to learning. While you sleep, old synapses are pruned, letting new ones grow. Writing is similar: when you dredge up a memory, part of it has rotted. Transcribing adds new threads and dyes. Writing about your life not only allows, but requires, you to change it.

In less tattered terms, writing about Eskild is a form of intellectual embalming. With my imagination running through his veins, he can stand up, shimmering, and walk. He can even talk, though I always know in advance what he's going to say.

Often, we'll set out on our usual ramble toward the ruins at Kronby. It's always summer here, under the birches along the dirt road of my mind. He slips his hand through mine. But of course it isn't really his. It's less his each time.

> When the ship parted, she had seen him sink into the deep waves, and she was glad, for she thought he would now be with her; and then she remembered that human beings could not live in the water, so that when he got down to her father's palace he would be quite dead.

"The man in the casket was a stranger to me," I wrote in an earlier draft. At the time of his wedding, I hadn't seen Eskild for six years, since my parents moved our family back to Utah in order to prevent their children, passing through the vales of adolescence, from encountering religious doubt.

Constant vigilance was required to keep a Mormon from sinking in the sea of secular Swedes. We did it mostly by banning things. If our laws seemed capricious, that's how we knew they were divine. God diverged from common sense at the crucial moment to remind us that The Word of Wisdom was about Him, not our health. We had meat only in winter, alcohol only in cake. We had a lot of cake. While tobacco was sinful, smoking in general was merely a bad idea. Tea was forbidden, but not (explicitly) pot.

To the scriptural bans, Mom added one of her own, which did more than all the rest to set us apart: no TV. Instead, we read aloud, finishing a book or two each month. The most memorable were Lindgren and Jansson, Dickens and Dumas, Wodehouse and Austen, but also *Tess of the d'Urbervilles*, *Madame Bovary*, *Anna Karenina*, *The Little Mermaid* —a DVD of Dvorak's *Rusalka*, too, when I was older—which kindled my interest in watery graves.

Like Rusalka, I'd have drowned my prince.

Our pop culture illiteracy did help prevent us from making friends at school, but Mom's plan backfired in profounder ways. No other children understood what Eskild and I thought was cool, least of all other Mormons. By the time I was thirteen, I realized the Book of Mormon was not good. I couldn't imagine Herr Settembrini or Naphtha from *The Magic Mountain* giving it a second thought. The people in my head were far cleverer than me—perhaps the main benefit of reading literature to a child.

Despite growing up in an affectionate family, part of a strong religious community, in perhaps the kindliest country on Earth, I always felt surrounded by enemies: Philistines.

I must have been unbearable, yet Eskild bore me. In the summer, there were a dozen places we could go to spend the day with my CD Walkman and his backpack full of books.

Grandma's yard, the arboretum, the riverside park . . . Best of all, though, were "the ruins at Kronby." There were rarely any tourists there, because the ruins were just lumps in the grass. But the grass was soft, and the lumps were boy-shaped. The shade from the willows tickled your face. There was a drainage canal—we called it "the moat"—where you could always find little fish, sunlight drizzling their shadows like honey.

For a while, after I emigrated, we kept in touch by email. Unfortunately, this was at the time when I was learning to "turn phrases." I remember saying I was "by nature monogamous to the point of celibacy." I meant this as a send-up of my narcissism—Eskild had always been disgusted by my admiration of my looks. But it was also a (vain) promise of fidelity: *I can imagine anything, except replacing you.*

She was a strange child, quiet and thoughtful; and while her sisters would be delighted with the wonderful things which they obtained from the wrecks of vessels, she cared for nothing but her pretty red flowers, like the sun, excepting a beautiful marble statue. It was the representation of a handsome boy, carved out of pure white stone, which had fallen to the bottom of the sea from a wreck.

In the first edition, Andersen's little mermaid, refusing to murder her prince, jumps into the sea and dissolves. In response to outraged readers, Andersen allowed her bubbles to rise and join the "daughters of the air," in whose company she can earn a soul after three centuries of good works, a term lengthened or abbreviated according to the good behavior of children.

In my opinion, this ending is even sadder than the first.

Our favorite game was make-believe. Most weekends, we'd sleep over at Grandma's. She'd read us stories at night, and the next morning, we'd act them out, using her impressive collection of dress-up clothes. I played the girls, Eskild the boys. There was never any question about this. We were both happy as long as the story contained a sword fight and a suicide.

One summer, Eskild had sailed far out onto Storsjön when a storm rolled in. The sky turned brown, the wind blew black. We were all sitting on the porch, watching, when his sail curled like one whitecap into the next. Some jet-skiers rescued him before Dad even had time to start our boat. Eskild's dinghy washed to shore a month later. Aside from the missing centerboard, it still worked. It still works, though the sail is tinted green.

Mom read to us the most, in terms of number of hours, but her voice came from Grandma. Everyone in my family inherited the Voice, to some degree. We play it in different keys and at different speeds, but the underlying melody is the same: a mixture of Jämtland dialect, Julie-Andrews-stars-in-*Fargo,* and the congenitally high palate that puts me in danger of the question "So, where are you from?" virtually anywhere in the world.

My siblings only use Grandma's voice when reading aloud, embarrassed, or frightened. Apparently, I sound like I'm reading aloud all the time.

Often, in the morning hours, the five sisters would twine their arms round each other, and rise to the surface, in a row. They had more beautiful voices than any human being could have; and before the approach of a storm, and when they expected a ship would be lost, they swam before the vessel, and sang sweetly of the delights to be found in the depths of the sea, begging the sailors not to fear if they sank to the bottom. But the sailors could not understand the song, they took it for the howling of the storm.

Swedish school was OK. At least I shared some classes with Es-kild. But in Mount Nash Junior High, walking down the halls, I often thought without irony of the little mermaid, for whom every step on dry land felt like the blade of a knife.

Is Andersen really nicer than the Grimm brothers? The latter reserve their red-hot slippers for ugly stepsisters.

Few people would admit to being ugly stepsisters in the stories of their own lives.

A few months before my family moved, Eskild's homework was to draw his "dream house," labelling every part in English. We sat by Grandma's pond, his notebook open on the grass.

"Are you sure 'Television's Room' makes sense?" I said.

"Of course, we'd mostly be watching opera on DVD . . ."

"What do you need so many bedrooms for?" I asked.

"One for me, one for each of my children," he said. "And one for you."

That was just how the future was going to be.

Eskild shared my exile in the Temple of Art, but he kept a few connections on the outside. For instance, Stig and Lars from church. They'd talk about soccer and missions and things in voices that filled me with envy and fear. Sometimes, we'd play Xbox at Stig's house: bloody, forbidden games in which I took my full share of the fun, especially since Eskild made me a sort of mascot, setting the example of laughing at my squeamish remarks: "What a picturesque effect the blood makes against the falling snow!"

It's important, in so many situations, to have someone to set the example of kindly laughter.

There was a time, though, when you'd have thought Eskild didn't like me at all. Perhaps we'd played *The Little Mermaid* once too often. There even came a day—distressing as it is to remember—when I thought there were tiny fish frozen in Grandma's pond while Eskild remained skeptical.

The sun hit Eskild's bed first, but he just turned over, nestling deeper into his pillow, letting me win the first, best game of the day: the race to Grandma's bed. I jumped in and squirmed, waiting for my cold toes to provoke her comment, usually something about icicles or "hard black rubber."

A few minutes later, Eskild would join us, pretending not to hurry, as if he didn't care I'd won. We'd doze for half an hour till Grandma pulled herself free. Eskild and I would slide into the warm hollow she'd left and watch while she applied makeup at the mirror. Our faces all blinked back—we her fuzzy shoulder angels, or if you changed focus, she the blurry troll between us. We didn't usually talk much in the mornings, but Grandma might have remarked that years ago her eyebrows, lips, or lashes had been as real as our own.

We'd eat toast with home-canned raspberries on top: "real raspberries," Grandma bragged, of a kind you couldn't buy in stores, because they were grey. Then we'd gather on the sofa for our morning session of reading aloud.

Nothing gave her so much pleasure as to hear about the world above the sea. She made her old grandmother tell her all she knew of the ships and of the towns, the people and the animals. To her it seemed most wonderful and beautiful to hear that the flowers of the land should have fragrance, and not those below the sea;

that the trees of the forest should be green; and that the fishes among the trees could sing so sweetly, that it was quite a pleasure to hear them. Her grandmother called the little birds fishes, or she would not have understood her; for she had never seen birds.

On this particular morning, Grandma released a word that floated around, like a piece of demon glass from *The Snow Queen*, until it stuck in Eskild's eye, changing the way he saw everything, or at least me. "Don't be sentimental," she'd said, slamming the book shut when I began to cry at the mermaid's plight:

"So I shall die," said the little mermaid, "and as the foam of the sea I shall be driven about never again to hear the music of the waves, or to see the pretty flowers nor the red sun. Is there anything I can do to win an immortal soul?"

"No," said the old woman, "unless a man were to love you so much that you were more to him than his father or mother (. . .) Then his soul would glide into your body and you would obtain a share in the future happiness of mankind (. . .) But this can never happen. Your fish's tail, which amongst us is considered so beautiful, is thought on earth to be quite ugly."

Grandma said she'd finish the story later if I promised to control myself.

"*I* wasn't crying," Eskild pointed out.

"No," she stroked his head. "That's my good boy."

Over the years, Grandma put Eskild and me through a course in emotional weight-training: *The Little Match Girl*, *The Little Mermaid*, even *Little Dorrit*. No matter how tragic the narrative became, only Grandma was allowed to cry—or rather let the throb into her voice that sometimes made even Eskild bite his lips or wander over to the window to look out at something bright.

Grandma probably just resented us for cheapening her feelings.

I know that's why I prefer recorded music to actual concerts, where there's always the danger of one's neighbor beginning to weep silently or conduct the orchestra in his lap.

Sentimentality only seems evil to people who view their emotions as a means of truth. It is an aesthete's sin. Perhaps Eskild got so angry about the fish because he wanted them to exist even more than I did. After all, if I was the one who cried at Grandma's stories, he was the one who lay still and listened.

The sun rose above the waves, and his warm rays fell on the cold foam of the little mermaid, who did not feel as if she were dying. She saw the bright sun, and all around her floated hundreds of transparent beautiful beings; she could see through them the white sails of the ship, and the red clouds in the sky; their speech was melodious, but too ethereal to be heard by mortal ears, as they were also unseen by mortal eyes.

It was exceptionally cold that afternoon. We were sweeping the snow off Grandma's pond to make a skating rink when I noticed something odd in the ice. I knelt down and blew on the surface, rubbing it clear:

Minnows! They'd been caught mid twitch, sides shimmering like tin. "How beautiful!" I said.

Eskild marched over, the word *sentimental* still gleaming in his eye. "What is it now?"

"Minnows—don't you see? There's a whole flock of them."

"It's called a *shoal*." But he was hooked. He ran to Grandma's shed to fetch everything sharp.

For hours, we hacked with hatchets and screwdrivers, prying out blocks that teemed with fish as long as they remained part of the pond, but turned clear when lifted up against the sky.

I feared the wee beasts had been shattered by our hammering.

Eskild threw down his hatchet in disgust. His cheeks were red, not just with cold. He'd been working much harder than I.

"I don't believe there ever were any," he said, heading toward the house.

"Wait—" I chipped out one last block.

This time the silver bits remained. Not just curds of frozen air—you could almost make out their gills.

Eskild took the block into the kitchen and dumped it in a pan. He turned the stove on high.

"You'll kill them!" I said.

He looked at me.

"Don't you know they're already dead?"

I couldn't watch; if you watched, they'd disappear.

I watched anyway, standing by Eskild, saying nothing until long after the water had begun to boil.

At first, everything did disappear. Just scum, dirt, bubbles—nothing more.

But if you look hard enough, you can see anything in a pot of water. A fin. Tiny eyes. Scales tumbling like leaves in the wind. Everything just a little too small to be certain of . . .

"I guess they melted," I said. "After all, their bodies were 99.9% water. But they were really there!"

I'm not sure I believed in the fish myself. But if Eskild would join my delusion of his own free will, that would be even better than a pot full of boiled minnows.

He listened to me, head tilted slightly, then grabbed the pot and marched outside. With a lifting motion, he poured the water out on the cement. It reared up in a white column, making him stagger. We watched the figures writhe over the treetops and into the sky.

We ran inside to boil more water.

What if we poured it in a circle? he suggested. Or a line of small drops? He rummaged through Grandma's pots, already devising the rules for a game beautiful enough to hold off doubt for one more day.

The Guest on Summer Island

Now the back end says, "Which way should I grow out? Should I make a new tail, or should I make a new head? Should I go on following and never have to make any important decisions, or should I be the one who always knows best, until I come apart again? That would be exciting."

—TOVE JANSSON, *The Summer Book*

· I ·

JUNE, 1935

And for once the Baltic was blue, crisscrossed with whitecaps and checkered with foam. The ferry was packed, it seemed, with huge flightless birds, not particularly excited about returning home. The sun brought them squinting out on deck; the wind made them huddle along a bench that might as well have been slatted with bone. Hands in pockets, bags between feet, the Ålanders shrank into the space between their own shoulders and looked out to sea. Occasionally, one of them made a remark and the girl strained her ears to catch it. But it was swallowed by the roar of the engine or the rolling of something in the hold.

Astrid wanted to ask her father what it was. But he was writing in his notebook. She wanted to ask Grandma where the other fathers were.

Why were Island People all so young or so old? But Grandma hadn't been responding well to questions lately.

Astrid didn't have so many questions, really. Just the one:

Why can't Ida join us for the summer?

Well, why couldn't she?

Ida had the most beautiful hair in school, and probably the world. She didn't mind if Astrid combed it. She didn't mind if Astrid pretended, for short periods, to be Ida. True, Ida was scared of ants and didn't know how to swim, but Astrid could have *taught* her—she clenched her fists. She could have found the ants' nest and drowned it in gasoline.

The other fathers, she decided, must have stayed on the mainland to work. Not everyone was smart enough to be a famous writer like Mr. Boberg.

How he hated to be distracted while he was writing! She was more than a little proud of the fact. Under the roar of the engine, however, she could sing without distracting anyone. She hardly even moved her lips:

> *My name is Ida*
> *and this is my song;*
> *it's not very long.*

She tapped her heels on the bar under her seat, counting the islands as they passed.

Depending on how big you required an island to be, there were between fifty and fifty thousand islands in Astrid's archipelago. Some were red and lumpy, mere piles of sunbaked clay. Others were chalky flats of mattress grass, rippling in their bluish way. Often, the birches rose straight out of the sea, it seemed, until you noticed the waves beneath them were made of stone.

The ferry crossed a sunken street, jagged roofs to either side. Astrid tried to make eye contact with the eiders in their nests, but they were too far away. She couldn't even see them blink, if that's what they were doing. But she could smell their poo.

Now and then, a house appeared: orange, green, or blue. A man was climbing a ladder, holding a pot of paint.

Astrid's own Red House lay far away. Tonight, she'd have to sleep at Cousin Anne's in Mariehamn. She'd be asked to play her *Träumerei*, and Dad would blame the weather for her mistakes. It warped the soundboard, cracked the keys.

She'd lie awake in the steep-pitched room, getting tangled in Grandma's snores. Why did the wallpaper smell like matches, but only when you looked? Until suddenly it would be morning, and the whole house would smell like pancakes, which Anne made with eggs and sour cream.

While Dad drained the fluid from their boat, Grandma would take Astrid to the navy store for jam, sardines, barrels of oats and beans, *knäckbröd*, canned butter, and *kryddost*. The beautiful boy behind the till would fill their gas tanks and roll them down the pier. Dad would be having a hard time starting the motor, which made Astrid feel ashamed. It would snuffle like a pig, blowing exhaust into the water, and she'd reach down to touch the fish that swarmed around the posts, mistaking the silver-brown bubbles for food.

Gradually, she'd begin to see the fish themselves as bubbles, rising from the nostrils of something vast. She'd run back to the center of the pier, making it sway on its pontoons, and look straight up till all she saw were clouds.

These, too, became monsters if you looked at them long enough. But nice, slow ones covered in fur.

Everything went as usual this year, except that Astrid forgot her *Dreams* halfway through, the boy at the till was replaced by a man, and Dad got the boat started right away. It idled out to sea, stopping with a jerk at the end of its rope.

"Hop in!" he shouted, hair flapping in the wind.

Cousin Anne waved goodbye. She always declined their invitation to come along. Really, after all these years, it would've been awkward if she'd said yes.

"There isn't really room for a guest on Summer Island," Grandma had explained, months ago. "At first, you'd love having Ida there, to comb her hair and show her everything for the first time. But then you'd begin to hate her for not having a place of her own. And she would feel scared with nowhere to hide."

And Astrid hadn't even divulged Ida's most shameful secret.

She was afraid of the sea.

You could almost jump from Åland onto Sommarö. In a pinch, anyway, you could swim. Dad hugged the coast all the way around. The cliffs turned red, the trees turned white. Soon, Mariehamn was out of sight. Astrid stared into the boat's churning wake—a rainbow hovered in the spray—and asked, "What happens if our propeller hits a fish?"

"What do you think happens?" Grandma said.

As they passed Hovnes, Summer Island's only town, Astrid waved at strangers on the pier. Only fifty people lived here, yet they were all still strangers to her. Well, she knew the Knudsens, at least by sight. A mile from Red House, they kept a farm year-round. But their children were all too old.

Between the forest and the sea, Red House seemed to have the island to itself. You could spend all summer there without seeing anyone.

It was wonderful, Grandma said.

Dad said so, too.

At last, they rounded Red House Point. The mountain looked taller from here. The water seemed smoother in its reflection.

"Hell," Dad said.

The dock was gone again. First, the ice must have bitten through its spindly legs, then carried it out and swallowed it whole. Even years the dock survived, Astrid could make out teeth marks in the wood. The ice gnawed the rock all the way around the island, leaving a rough ring, sometimes lower, sometimes higher. Sometimes very high indeed.

Dad hoisted the motor and ran the boat aground. Astrid hopped out before the gravel had stopped squeaking. She didn't even get her feet wet.

The garden was the first thing she ran to see. It was most like people waiting for her. But the leaves were still too small to hide the trees, which all bent in the same direction. One held an uprooted lilac in its arms.

Astrid wished she could stay here during the winter, at least once, to see the storms.

She wasn't much help with the cleanup, just carried small things in from the boat then trailed around after Dad and Grandma, watching them work.

First, Dad wheeled the water tank up the hill and filled it with rainwater from the cistern. He had to start the siphon by mouth. It tasted, he said, like spinach. When they got back to the house, he filled a glass and placed it on a sheet of paper. The algae showed up like a puff of green smoke.

"Some type of charophyte," he said. "Very nutritious."

Next, he cleared out the chimney with a long-handled brush. An egg tumbled onto the hearth. Its shell was pink and its yolk was the size of a marble. Astrid studied it for traces of bird.

"Are you sad?" Dad asked.

"It just looks normal," she said. She knew she was saying something wrong.

Dad laughed. He picked apart the egg, explaining what he was doing as he spread the inner, outer, and vitelline membranes over his thumb. He peeled off the germinal disc and lifted up the snotty chalazae, white protein ropes that held the yolk in place. "A typical eggshell contains seven thousand pores," he said. "Throughout incubation, these openings let in oxygen and release carbon dioxide, much like your lungs."

"No," Astrid said. She didn't like the idea of a breathing egg. She went to help Grandma sweep the dead flies out of the kitchen and peel the storm-paper off the windows. Then they wandered through the house to see what the Kraul had stolen this year.

In a way, the Kraul was their nearest neighbor. He lived on Screaming Gull Skerry, less than a mile from shore. But you could never see him on account of the mist. A few years ago, he had just shown up, squatting in the concrete hut where the lighthouse keeper and his wife had died. The hut was chained to the rock on all four corners and had one round window, which must offer the best possible view of waves during a storm. Perhaps you could even watch the fish swim by.

The Kraul had a bright new boat, but you never saw him lay out nets. He caught his fish one at a time, by pole, and must get awfully tired of them, Astrid thought, which was perhaps why he came to Summer Island to forage. At least, he was the prime suspect in the Case of the Disappearing Cloudberries.

Grandma wouldn't begrudge anyone a few apples or windfall pears. Such things were free for the taking, as if by natural law. But cloudberries—they grew only in the wild, and could only be gathered once a year. In shops, they cost a fortune, but the main thing—though it often went unsaid—was their magic strength. Without cloudberries, at her age, Grandma would undoubtedly be dead.

Last July, Summer Island's patch had borne a bumper crop: three gallons, Grandma had guessed, licking her coral lips. But on the morning when the berries should have turned definitively to gold, Astrid had found the vines stripped clean by clumsy fingers.

Or beaks—Dad had tried to blame the theft on birds. When Grandma ordered him to evict the Kraul, he had protested this would be unkind. Where was the Kraul supposed to go? True, he looked unsavory: cod-faced, glass eyes—the kind of fisherman who always wears a hat. Astrid was encouraged to avoid him.

This wasn't hard.

But she couldn't help thinking about him sometimes.

She wished she knew more exactly what he looked like.

At last, Grandma's search brought them to the guest room bureau, where leftover, mismatched things gathered and grew more beautiful with time. There was a book of silhouettes Grandma had painted as a girl, lenses for a telescope that no longer existed, a bone, a queen of spades, a Russian tambourine . . .

"What would the Kraul want with our junk?" Astrid asked—quietly, because Dad, through the wall, was already singing the Mozart that meant he was Onto Something.

"Is *this* junk?" Grandma asked, holding up the walrus fan as if Astrid had never seen it before. She splayed its yellow blades, revealing coastlines, ships, and dog-head whales, splashing through the grain of the bone. On the leftmost edge, a bearded serpent smiled straight out at you. "That's how Uncle Jonas signed his name."

Grandma began to reminisce about winters as a child. Some years, the ice froze so thick you could walk all the way to the lighthouse at Screaming Gull Skerry. Ringed seals lived in the snowbanks then. With all the Summer Folk arriving, though, Grandma couldn't blame them for leaving.

Aren't we Summer Folk?—Astrid knew better than to ask.

While Grandma continued talking, Astrid planned to have a large family—something she often did. Six daughters, three sons. The eldest would be Ingrid, Jonas. For the others, something English, something French . . . She'd always liked *Ivan*. Finnish names, too, like words played on a flute and drum. If only she had some Finnish blood!

None of them could be called Ida. Yet Ida would be involved, somehow. She would hover over the creation of Astrid's children in the manner of a pink cloud.

Grandma was still talking. Astrid sat on the rope-bed, making it creak. The guest room had been tacked on to the back of the house, continuing the slant of the roof so it almost touched the ground. The window was too big, and the floor was always cold because there used to be a bog underneath. Dad had filled it with sand and covered it with grass, but it still exhaled a farty mist.

If Ida had slept here, Astrid reflected, she might have gotten sick.

· 11 ·

The next morning, Astrid and Grandma set out early to see the island before Dad woke up. Grandma probably would have gone without Astrid, too, if she'd been able to wake up early enough. The sky was clear, the meadow full of harebells and mayweed, spring flowers that might last all summer here. Grandma picked up a dead bird by the wingtips and threw it into a bush.

Astrid wandered out along the promontory where Dad liked to dive. The rock dropped away in steps, green then blue, fringed with seaweed whose undulation seemed to be happening at the backs of your own eyes.

She shivered and went to swim in the pond instead, where she could touch the bottom, and the scariest creatures were only tadpoles, leeches, skating-spiders, a kind of velvety backswimmer that liked to chase people, and snakes. The only real downside was the water was too dirty to open your eyes in.

Crawling out, she grabbed a stone. The sucking, as it came loose, lasted too long. It felt like a potato wrapped in plaster, and wore a bright green skirt. She touched it with her tongue. Such rocks were sometimes full of garnets, and she took it home so Dad could split it open for her.

But Dad's typewriter was in full swing, so she laid the stone on her bed, where it watched while she drew sperm whales being eaten by seahorses. That night, it listened while she said her prayers, and by the next morning, it had acquired a personality—silent, but full of sympathy, an excellent listener—and Astrid decided to name it Melisande, the most aristocratic name she could think of.

For several weeks, Astrid was happy with her new companion. She showed Melisande her poems and drawings. She taught her the names of island flowers. She took her on safari in the birch thicket, where Melisande helped to kill a lot of dangerous red ants.

But soon, Astrid began to realize that Melisande didn't have everything she wanted in a friend. Arms, for instance, and legs. But Astrid knew that if you looked hard enough, you could find anything you needed on the island. Or else, one day, it would wash ashore.

She searched the beach for arms and legs to tape to Melisande so she would seem more human in bed. Gull bones were about the right size, and she'd stuffed her shirt with them when she stumbled over a tuft of grass and dropped them all.

The grass was long and fine, bleached by the sun, and Astrid saw at once it would make the perfect wig. Melisande didn't need legs. After all, where would she go? All she needed was hair.

Astrid uprooted the grass and carried it home. She cut off the roots, squeezed a pile of glue onto Melisande's head, and pressed the grass into it. She forced herself not to touch the wig all day, and by the next morning, it was attached so firmly, she could run her fingers through it without dislodging a straw. She was so pleased with her friend's new beauty, she wrote a poem for her and read it aloud:

> *There is a rock hight Melisande*
> *Of which I'm fond.*
> *I found her by an azure pond*
> *But now she's blonde,*
> *Hooray!*

· III ·

Toward the beginning of August, Dad went to Mariehamn to check the mail and buy groceries. The trip would take all afternoon, and Astrid asked Grandma if the time had come, at last, to surprise Dad with a cloudberry pie.

"Perhaps," Grandma said, sniffing the air. "But don't touch anything until I get there."

From far away, Astrid could tell the berries were gone. Just by the way the leaves fluttered. She skirted the scene, hardly daring to go near. Huge footprints led down to the shore, vanishing at the wrack line. As if the Kraul had dissolved into the waves!

It was strange they hadn't heard his boat.

It was strange Grandma hadn't smelled him coming.

Had he swum? Or simply walked?

"What a monster," Astrid said admiringly.

"He's not getting away with it this time," Grandma said.

Astrid followed her back to the house. But instead of going in, Grandma began tugging the rowboat down to the shore. She seemed to grow a little angrier with each tug.

"What are you doing?" Astrid asked. She didn't expect an answer.

Grandma suffered from fits of hatred and mischief. The best thing to do was go along and try to keep her out of trouble. Astrid hopped into the prow. Grandma rolled onto the back seat and began pulling jerkily at the oars. The boat spun for a while before settling in the only direction it could possibly take.

The waves were sharp but small. Now and then, one showered Astrid's back. She considered many comments before she finally said, "Lovely day."

Grandma grunted as if rowing hurt her back.

Screaming Gull Skerry came closer and closer, surrounded by foam.

The Kraul's boat was gone.

"He must be out fishing!" Astrid said. Now they'd have to turn around. It was unthinkable to land on someone else's island when he wasn't home.

Grandma seemed to hesitate. Then her eyes narrowed.

There was a sign in the gravel: "No Trespassing."

"Get out," Grandma said.

They dragged the boat ashore. Grandma was smiling unpleasantly, as if practicing for the Kraul.

"We're just going to see if he has my berries," she said. "That's all."

The Kraul's hut was closed with a padlock. There wasn't even a key hanging by the door. This made Astrid feel better when Grandma used her knife to remove the screws. The padlock fell to pieces on the rocks.

"Ordinarily, of course, you should never do this," Grandma said as she passed into the room.

It was surprisingly cozy: walls bright with lime, a patchwork rug under a red metal bed, a floral easy chair, and a bookcase full of books. On the far wall, a rack was covered with tackle and houseplants. The biggest thing was an oily table the Kraul had presumably built himself out of driftwood. Astrid picked up a bowl made of the same shimmering material, but put it down with a clunk when Grandma said, "Shh!"

Grandma sneaked up on the cupboard and opened it suddenly, as if hoping to find the Kraul inside.

There were the cloudberries, dripping with light.

"Ah!" Grandma said.

At any moment, Astrid expected to hear heavy feet.

"Can we go now?" she said.

"In a minute," Grandma said. "I need to catch my breath." She placed the basket by the door and collapsed into the easy chair. "So soft!" she said, and pulled a book from the shelf. "Agatha Christie, *The Secret Adversary*," she said approvingly. "I'm surprised the Kraul knows English." She crossed her legs and began to read.

Astrid wandered around, touching things. Most memorably a photo of two men and a baby, presumably grandfather, father, and son. They looked so healthy and Finnish—mistrustful, yet eager to confide. Could any of them be the Kraul?

She lay on the bed and closed her eyes. It smelled like Stockholm. Someone seemed to be draping blankets over her, as thin as smoke.

She heard the sound of the motor long before she realized what it was.

"He's back!" she said, tearing herself awake.

Grandma looked around, mouth open, as if dazed by her impending shame.

"The birches!" Astrid grabbed Grandma's hand and pulled her to-ward the door. Grandma kicked over the cloudberries and stepped in them. She was still clutching her book.

The birch thicket lay about fifty yards behind the house. Astrid had trouble prying her way in, but found a sort of tunnel behind a dock leaf. She crawled until she could stand. Then, noticing moss beneath her, she fell.

The birches were so tangled, only scraps of sky shone through. She heard Grandma crashing through the branches.

"Over here!" Astrid croaked.

Grandma padded over and laid her smutty face next to Astrid's. They panted.

They laughed.

"Shh!" Astrid said.

The sound of the motor had stopped.

"Maybe he didn't see our boat," Astrid said.

Grandma spread out her arms, as if to keep herself from rolling down a hill.

Astrid was beginning to feel pleasantly in charge of the adventure.

"We'll just have to wait till nightfall, then sneak away," she said. "Do you want one of your pills?" She rummaged through Grandma's pockets and found a mint. "Open wide," she said, placing it on Grandma's lips.

The sunlight was filtering through the branches, spattering every-thing with squares. At this time of year, there was no such thing as nightfall, really, and Astrid was beginning to get cold.

"This is ridiculous," Grandma said. She brushed some leaves out of her hair. "I'm not staying here all day."

"I'll go see what he's doing," Astrid said. "Will you be alright without me?"

Grandma grunted. She opened her book, squinted, and turned it right-side up.

Somehow, getting out of the forest was easier than going in. Astrid flitted—flitting seemed to make the gravel squeak less—to the back of the Kraul's hut. As the sun passed behind a wave of clouds, every color blued. Her heart thumped inside her chest. She was terrified in a way that was more amusing than anything she had felt before.

The Kraul was crouching in front of a camp stove, his face lit from below. The brim of his hat stuck out like a giant nose. He was throwing something into a bucket over and over again.

He began talking to someone. His Finnish accent made him sound playful, almost Russian. After a while, she realized the Kraul was speaking to her.

"Yes, you—Miss Trespasser. Why don't you come and say hi?"

Whatever was in the Kraul's bucket, it was splashing.

It was frogs.

The Kraul was cutting them in half. He took them out of the bucket one at a time, squeezing them tightly as they kicked the air. He grabbed them under the shoulders and carved off their legs with a single stroke. He tossed the legs into the pan and dropped the front parts on the ground, where they kept twitching. Just nerves, probably. One in particular stared at Astrid, gulping for air. Its lungs lay beside it on the gravel.

"Can you stab that one again?" she asked.

"Of course," the Kraul said, then began on the next frog.

"Why don't you kill them *before* you cut their legs off?" Astrid asked.

The Kraul just laughed. He shook the pan to keep the legs from burning and turned down the flame.

"Where did you find all those?" Astrid asked.

The Kraul seemed not to hear.

"Where's your grandmother hiding?" he asked.

"She's not hiding," Astrid said coolly. "She's taking a nap in the woods. Today has been rather fatiguing for her. God I never saw such big frogs."

She heard footsteps. She and the Kraul turned to watch Grandma approach. Her knees and elbows were stained with mud, but her face wore an expression of great dignity.

The Kraul rose to greet her, taking off his hat. Underneath, his grey hair was surprisingly thick.

"Mrs. Boberg..." he said.

"I came to inquire if I could borrow a book," Grandma said, holding out the Agatha Christie. Its cover was spattered with mud. "As you were out, we thought the polite thing would be—"

"Yes, yes," the Kraul said, cutting her off. "What exactly were you looking for?" He seemed willing to let Grandma off easy, so Astrid was horrified when he added, "I must say, you Summer Folk have odd ideas about private property."

"My cloudberries!" Grandma screamed. "Where are they?"

The Kraul stared.

"You're always stealing from us!" Grandma went on. "We never see you, but we know you're there! Filching, lying, sneaking, stinking!" She took a deep breath. "I was going to make a cloudberry pie for Mr. Boberg, you see. It's his favorite."

"I'm sorry," the Kraul said, turning his hat over in his hands. "I didn't know... I gather stuff from all the islands around here. I thought that's what Island People do."

"Island People," Grandma said triumphantly, "don't lock their doors. They don't put up signs." She walked over to the "No Trespassing" sign and kicked it. She lost her balance and had to sit down.

Astrid rushed over. Grandma was laughing noiselessly to herself. She ignored Astrid and took the Kraul's outstretched hands.

"Won't you come inside for a cup of tea?" he asked.

"I've caused enough trouble," Grandma said, dusting off her dress. "We'd better be getting home so Mr. Boberg doesn't find an empty house."

"But you must be exhausted!" the Kraul said. "After such a busy day."

"Can I have a frog?" Astrid asked.

They smelled wonderful, more like bread than fish. The current batch was beginning to burn.

"Of course. They're best fresh." He held the door open. Crossing the threshold, Grandma stepped over the basket of smashed berries without even mentioning it.

The gas lamp and stove warmed up the Kraul's hut. Soon, the teapot was unspooling a ribbon of steam. The Kraul served the frogs' legs in a pool of butter on a huge plate, and set the example of eating with his hands.

Astrid picked one up by the toes. She had to close her eyes before she could bite—it looked so human. But the meat was soft as cantaloupe, and soon she was eating another.

"I hope you'll forgive me for stealing your frogs," the Kraul said. "When you live here all winter, you start to think of the islands as your own."

"Yes, I know," Grandma said. "My family has lived here for more than a hundred years."

"And to think, I considered myself a native!" the Kraul said.

A little patronizingly, Astrid thought, but Grandma relaxed, and when he asked her, "How did your family stay busy all winter?" she began to tell him.

He got down a bottle of whiskey and poured a glass for himself and another for Grandma. He poured one for Astrid, too, but Grandma intercepted it.

He kept refilling their glasses as they talked, and Astrid sat silently and watched, proud and astonished to hear her grandmother speaking so freely.

At one point, the Kraul turned to Astrid.

"Next summer, you must meet my grandson," he said. "His name is Leksi and he's as pretty as a girl. Not much older than you, I'd guess. Well, I haven't seen him for a while . . . He's coming here next summer to learn to fish. His father, too."

Tears had formed in the Kraul's eyes. He turned his head. "He doesn't have many friends. I guess it runs in the family . . . You shouldn't argue with your children," he said to Grandma. She changed the conversation to hunting and gathering.

"Last year," the Kraul said thickly, "I turned your cloudberries into a wonderful pot of cloudberry jam." He got up and rummaged in the cupboard. "I hope you'll take some with your tea."

Grandma accepted a dollop straight into her whiskey. She stirred it with her finger, then took a sip.

"I must teach you how to make proper cloudberry jam," she said. "But first," she raised her finger, "I must put up a sign in our cloudberry patch: No Trespassing..."

The Kraul began to chuckle. Grandma smiled. They both began to laugh, shaking the table, and Astrid felt scared.

She thought of Dad coming home to an empty house. Where, he'd wonder, could they possibly have gone?

She wondered, too, what was the color of Leksi's hair.

· IV ·

Dear Ida,

I have been thinking about you a lot while you aren't here.

My grandmother has made a new friend.

My father has written a new book.

I even found a rock that looks like you! Don't be offended because it is very beautiful.

I thought I would say I found a swallow instead because that sounds less weird.

What are you doing this summer? I hope your cat and brother are well.

—Astrid

Astrid couldn't think of any natural way to ask about Ida's hair. She hoped it was all still there.

She could have given Dad the letter, or walked to Hovnes and mailed it herself. But after all these months, she wasn't sure Ida was her friend any longer. She decided to take the letter back to school and give it to Ida by hand, if the time seemed right.

She suspected it never would.

· v ·

Toward the beginning of September, a fantastic storm arrived, straight from the Pole. Astrid sat in the window, watching the colors change. Her skin prickled at the first spatter on the glass.

Dad laid a hand on her head.

"Are you sad?" he asked. "Är du ledsen, min flicka?"

"Yes," she said, though her heart was wild with joy.

"So talented," Dad said. "And so sad!"

A gust shook the window and Astrid leaned against her father's side. She wanted to ask an intelligent question, but instead began to cry.

"I don't want to go back to school," she said. "But I guess there isn't any help for it?"

"No," Dad said, stroking her hair. "I guess there isn't."

The next morning, Astrid woke early in order to search the flotsam before the others could get to it. The sky was rough and low, like the ceiling of a cave. She took Melisande with her for courage.

Behind the cape, the storm had spun the reeds around each rock, so thick it looked like you could walk out onto them. Kelp pods rotated in the patches of open water, filling with morning light. A flock of gulls flew overhead, shrieking.

"They're going home," Astrid murmured, with a little spasm of sorrow.

She walked out to the end of the little promontory where Dad liked to dive, and took her clothes off. She sat on the rock, shivering. She found herself often here in dreams, but then her body was covered in blankets, so it didn't feel cold.

The water was so clear, no reflections at all! She combed Melisande's hair one last time, then pushed her in. Melisande bounced slowly from ledge to ledge, then was gone.

Astrid dove in after her. She kept her eyes open, but there wasn't much to see. Just the black-green rock, crystal chips, the swaying seaweed, the endless blue.

Whatever might be down there, now Melisande was, too.

The bubbles rose around Astrid's body like hundreds of transparent beautiful beings. The white sun fluttered on the waves like the sails of a ship. She did not feel as if she were dying.

When she was unable to hold her breath any longer, she rose to the surface and just floated.

THE IOWA SHORT FICTION AWARD AND THE JOHN SIMMONS SHORT FICTION AWARD WINNERS, 1970–2018

Donald Anderson
Fire Road
Dianne Benedict
Shiny Objects
Marie-Helene Bertino
Safe as Houses
Will Boast
Power Ballads
David Borofka
Hints of His Mortality
Robert Boswell
Dancing in the Movies
Mark Brazaitis
*The River of Lost Voices:
Stories from Guatemala*
Jack Cady
The Burning and Other Stories
Pat Carr
The Women in the Mirror
Kathryn Chetkovich
Friendly Fire

Cyrus Colter
The Beach Umbrella
Marian Crotty
What Counts as Love
Jennine Capó Cruce
How to Leave Hialeah
Jennifer S. Davis
Her Kind of Want
Janet Desaulniers
What You've Been Missing
Sharon Dilworth
The Long White
Susan M. Dodd
Old Wives' Tales
Merrill Feitell
*Here Beneath Low-Flying
Planes*
Christian Felt
The Lightning Jar
James Fetler
Impossible Appetites

Lex Williford
  Macauley's Thumb
Miles Wilson
  Line of Fall
Russell Working
  Resurrectionists

Charles Wyatt
  Listening to Mozart
Don Zancanella
  Western Electric